"Is this my son, Sabrina?"

So this was how it was going to be. She hadn't planned to tell him on a beautiful, sunny May day in front of the hometown crowd, but he'd asked. "Yes. Joe is your son."

Jonas studied the baby, and Joe seemed to study him in return. "I assume my name is listed as the father on the birth certificate?"

"Yes, it is. Of course it is." Sabrina took Joe back from his father, who seemed reluctant to part with his newfound son. "We have an appointment, Jonas. I'm sorry."

"What kind of appointment?"

"Six-month checkup and shots."

"I feel I should be there."

Sabrina stopped and looked up at the tall, handsome man whom she'd once loved with all her heart.

"I'm not trying to butt into your life, Sabrina. When Joe sees the doctor, I want to be there. Every time."

"Fine. You can hold him when he cries."

"He won't cry. He's a Callahan."

Dear Reader,

Jonas Callahan doesn't settle down easily! None of the brothers have, but Jonas is determined that he's meant to walk alone in life. Until he finds out that his longtime love is carrying his child—not another man's—and Jonas's world is forever changed. In the painted canyons of Diablo, New Mexico, Jonas is going to have to allow the magic that has swept the other brothers to finally find him. It's up to Jonas to change his own destiny and be the husband, father and Callahan he's meant to be. Fortunately, Sabrina McKinley is more than up to the challenge—this stubborn cowboy doctor is her dream come true!

I hope you've enjoyed this series. My editor and I spent many hours putting it together. It was so much fun writing about these wily brothers and their cagey counterparts—not to mention their crafty Aunt Fiona. Family is fun and magical in its own right, and though it takes the brothers some time to find their own true loves and families, the magic of Rancho Diablo eventually tames them all. It's my heartfelt wish that some of that special magic finds its way into your life, and as the Callahan cowboys ride into the New Mexico sunset, here's hoping they leave you with many smiles and much happiness.

Best wishes always,

Tina Leonard

www.tinaleonard.com

www.facebook/tinaleonardbooks

www.twitter/tina_leonard

A Callahan Wedding

TINA LEONARD

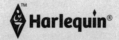

TORONTO NEW YORK LONDON
AMSTERDAM PARIS SYDNEY HAMBURG
STOCKHOLM ATHENS TOKYO MILAN MADRID
PRAGUE WARSAW BUDAPEST AUCKLAND

Recycling programs
for this product may
not exist in your area.

ISBN-13: 978-0-373-75405-2

A CALLAHAN WEDDING

Copyright © 2012 by Tina Leonard

This edition published by arrangement with Harlequin Books S.A.

For questions and comments about the quality of this book
please contact us at Customer_eCare@Harlequin.ca

® and TM are trademarks of the publisher. Trademarks indicated with
® are registered in the United States Patent and Trademark Office, the
Canadian Trade Marks Office and in other countries.

www.Harlequin.com

Printed in U.S.A.

ABOUT THE AUTHOR

Tina Leonard is a bestselling author of more than forty projects, including a popular thirteen-book miniseries for Harlequin American Romance. Her books have made the Waldenbooks, Ingram and Nielsen BookScan bestseller lists. Tina feels she has been blessed with a fertile imagination and quick typing skills, excellent editors and a family who loves her career. Born on a military base, she lived in many states before eventually marrying the boy who did her crayon printing for her in the first grade. Tina believes happy endings are a wonderful part of a good life. You can visit her at www.tinaleonard.com.

Books by Tina Leonard

HARLEQUIN AMERICAN ROMANCE

The Callahan Cowboys series has been so much fun to write! I have enjoyed every minute of these brothers' adventures, and for those moments of joy I must shower my gratitude on the following people: my editor, Kathleen Scheibling; all copy editors and other gurus of magic at Harlequin who are responsible for making my books the best they can be; my children, Lisa and Dean; my husband, Tim; agent Laura Bradford for negotiating this contract; and most of all, the readers who have loyally supported my work all these many years. Thank you so much.

Chapter One

"Jonas is an old soul."
—Molly Cavanaugh Callahan, observing her
toddler as he tried to read the newspaper one day,
imitating his father, Jeremiah.

Jonas Callahan realized at once that the music he heard on the breeze was the lilting strains of a wedding march, beautifully played as always by the town of Diablo's string quartet.

It had to come from Sam's wedding. Though Sam had already married Seton McKinley once, they'd probably decided to make the leap from marriage-by-design to marriage-by-dream-come-true. Sam was sentimental like that. Oh, Jonas's loony lawyer brother would claim he was a hard-boiled realist, but Sam was the biggest, cheesiest romantic of the entire Callahan clan. And a May wedding at Rancho Diablo was probably a dream come true—if one had romantic tendencies like that. Sam did. Jonas didn't.

He dared not intrude on the magical moment between his brother and Seton. Jonas knew full well how Sam had longed for her—as Jonas did for her sister, Sabrina.

While it was hopeless for him, Sam looked to be making everything happen for himself. Jonas was happy for his youngest brother, thrilled, in fact.

So Jonas stood near the English-style house with seven chimneys, where no one could see that he had come home to Rancho Diablo—and that he'd brought with him a visitor of the female variety.

"It's a wedding!" Chelsea Myers exclaimed. "I wouldn't mind getting married here—this place is gorgeous. Did you know there was a wedding today, Jonas?"

He shook his head. "I haven't been keeping in touch with my brothers as much as I should have. I sent an occasional email to let them know I didn't find our aunt and uncle, but that was about it."

Jonas craned his neck to see who was at the altar. It *was* Sam! For a man who'd run as hard as Sam had from the bonds of matrimony, he'd gone down like a sleepy baby when he'd met the right woman.

I'm too logical and practical to be led around by my heart. I intend to make my decision on cold, hard facts. Are we compatible? Does my future wife understand that I need an assistant in my life? I don't want romance and fairy tales and magic wedding gowns that can't possibly be magic. Sabrina and her load of clairvoyant, out-of-this-world supernatural charm.

Hooey!

Jonas, too, had met the woman he had once hoped might be the "right" one—but Sabrina McKinley had fallen for someone else. To say that his heart had broken upon learning that she was pregnant with another man's child would be grossly understating his devastation.

He'd had no option but to hightail it away from Rancho Diablo. He'd headed to Ireland on the flimsy excuse that he was going to locate their aunt Fiona and uncle Burke. When Jonas couldn't find them—it seemed they'd gotten a traveling yen and gone off on the extended cruise of their dreams—he'd hung around Ireland to take in the sights.

And then he'd met Chelsea Myers, a calm, steady redhead nothing like Sabrina McKinley—except for the flaming hair. Jonas had told himself she would make a suitable surgeon's wife. Moreover, she wasn't opposed to leaving Ireland and seeing America.

So, realizing that with Sam off the market, he'd be the only brother at Rancho Diablo who hadn't succumbed to Aunt Fiona's Secret Plan to get them all married with families, Jonas had surveyed his life goals. Now, he thought marriage might dovetail with his desire to not be the leftover Callahan, hankering after a woman who had borne another man's child.

What else could a guy with a broken heart do?

AFTER THE I DO'S WERE SAID and the champagne was flowing, Jonas stepped forward with Chelsea to join his brothers and congratulate Sam and Seton for finally doing things right this time.

"Jonas!" he heard over and over, glad cries of astonished welcome ringing in his ears. A burn of embarrassment crawled up the back of his neck. Sam's and Seton's big day was suddenly turning into a welcome home party for him.

"Brother," Sam said, hugging him and pounding him on the back. "Welcome home!"

"Congratulations, Sam. You've married a great gal. Again."

Seton threw her arms around Jonas and kissed him on the cheek like a long-lost brother. "You were gone too long! What a nice wedding gift to have you back!"

He suddenly realized he was staring at the maid of honor and the reason he'd left town: Sabrina. No longer pregnant, of course—he estimated her baby would be about six months old—Sabrina was dressed in a beautiful long, strapless, turquoise-blue dress that complemented her petite frame. Her burnished red hair was styled in a pretty updo, and her big eyes sparkled at him before her eyelids lowered.

Everything hit him all at once, a hard smack to the chest: He had never gotten over Sabrina. He was madly in love with her. And no matter how long he stayed away, no matter how many countries he traveled to, she was always going to be the one woman who set his soul on fire.

"Hi, Jonas," she said, and he felt himself melting at her feet.

"Hello, Sabrina. You look…nice." He'd started to say beautiful, but awkwardly stopped himself in time. "Congratulations, Seton, Sam."

"You ol' dog," Sam said. "We thought you were going to turn out to be the most footloose one of us all, going off like that. It's about time you came home!"

Jonas cleared his throat, knowing the moment had come. "I'd like everyone to meet my fiancée, Chelsea Myers."

For ten feet around him, it got so silent not even a grain of dirt shifted underfoot, or so Jonas's imagination feverishly claimed. He saw a flare of surprise in Sabrina's eyes that she quickly masked.

The moment was more painful than pleasant. Definitely not the self-serving, face-saving moment he'd hoped for.

It occurred to him belatedly that he wasn't as good at plotting as his aunt Fiona was, because at the moment, he felt anything but happy. Looking at Sabrina, he was pretty certain he'd made an error of epic proportions.

"Hi, Chelsea," Seton said. "Welcome to Rancho Diablo."

Sabrina moved forward to shake Chelsea's hand, but her aunt Corinne stepped in front of her, placing a baby in Sabrina's arms.

"I don't know why Joe's fussy," Corinne said, her voice merry. "Must want his mother."

The baby wasn't fussing. Jonas didn't think he'd ever seen a happier child. The infant had chubby cheeks, big blue eyes, a shock of black hair and a generous mouth that seemed to smile at everyone. Jonas chuckled. People said that babies smiled when they had gas, but this one just looked content. In fact, he'd seen a similar goofy, delighted smile on a baby before. Sam had grinned like that when he was an infant. Jonas remembered it clearly, because he'd been so shocked when a new baby appeared on the ranch after their parents had "gone to heaven."

Jonas had been old enough to know that a baby shouldn't come after parents died. Nevertheless, Sam had arrived one day, carried into the house by Fiona. The new baby had been the happiest kid on the planet. He'd smiled all the time, and the five brothers had been quite taken by what Fiona announced was their new brother.

Jonas found himself smiling back at Sabrina's happy baby in spite of himself—and then, like a lightning bolt sent from above, his brain cleared.

That was a *Callahan* smile. Those were Callahan navy-blue eyes. That was the black-as-night Callahan hair.

He looked at Sabrina, who was watching him with wide eyes. He glanced at Sam, then at Seton, then at his brother Rafe, who was playing best man. They all stared back at him in silence, and the curtain lifted on his self-denial.

This was *his* child.

The realization staggered him.

He had a son. A beautiful son. Jonas swallowed hard.

He couldn't help himself; he reached out to take the baby. The child came to him willingly, and Jonas felt unbidden tears jump into his eyes.

Holy smokes. I'm a father.

"What's his name?" he asked.

"I call him little Joe," Sabrina answered.

Jonas studied her, then looked down at the child in his arms. "Hi, little Joe."

The baby put a curled fist on Jonas's chin.

"He's a darling," Chelsea said. "Such a happy baby!"

Tears swam helplessly in Jonas's eyes. To cover his emotion, he handed the baby back to Sabrina. He realized that guests were milling around them, trying not to listen in, but this was Diablo, after all. Folks were curious about what was happening.

Jonas felt weak and somehow stupid. Poleaxed. "Congratulations," he said to Sabrina. "He…"

He started to say *doesn't have your beautiful red hair, he got my ordinary black,* and then choked back the words. Finally, he just nodded to his brothers and Seton and Sabrina, and hauled ass to the punch table.

Chelsea followed him. "Are you all right, Jonas?"

He worked to take in the deepest breath he could. "Yeah." But he didn't glance at her.

"Look, Jonas." She put a gentle hand on his forearm, and he turned to face her. "Under our agreement, which was nonbinding, all you asked for was a fiancée to help you save face. I agreed to that because I wanted to come to America, but I don't think it's working out the way you hoped it would."

He definitely hadn't saved any face. "Maybe not."

"You don't owe me anything, Jonas." Chelsea's eyes were soft. "It wasn't like we had a grand love affair. You've never even kissed me, other than as a sister."

"You're a nice woman, Chelsea. I like that about you. You're calm and steady, not like…" *Her.* Not like Sabrina, who kept him churned up, not knowing if she was a gypsy or a spy or a woman on a mission to destroy his heart.

"You're in love with her, Jonas. Anyone can see that." Chelsea smiled at him. "It looked like Cupid smacked you right on the nose with his quiver when you saw Sabrina. And when you held that baby—"

"Let's go for a drive," Jonas said. "I can't think about it. I want to get a whiskey at Banger's."

Chelsea shook her head. "Running off is not saving face. As I recall, that was your primary goal."

"You're right." He shook his head, trying to clear it from the mist of emotions clouding his brain. "Did you see that baby?" he asked, unable to believe his denseness. How could he not have ever suspected that Sabrina was pregnant with his child?

And everyone had known but him.

"I did see little Joe," Chelsea said dryly. "He looks just like you. How much you want to bet that Joe is short for Jonas?"

He blinked. "I doubt it."

She laughed. "Jonas, as the daughter of your aunt's neighbor in Ireland, I feel I have a little leeway to tell you not to be such a hardhead. Why were you so intent on believing she wasn't having your baby? I distinctly remember you saying that it nearly killed you when you came home for your brother's last wedding, and she was sticking out like a house. That's what you said—that she was sticking out like a house. Did it never occur to you to simply ask her?" Chelsea asked softly.

"I didn't want to hear the answer," he said. "I was so sure she'd found someone when she moved to Washington, D.C. Chelsea, I've done you a terrible disservice."

"Not me," she said, laughing. "I'm having a great time. I'm sorry you're suffering, though. Listen, I hate to leave you moldering here at the punch bowl, but I'm starved. Will you mind if I head over to the buffet table and grab a plate?"

He shook his head, feeling lost and thick. Really thick. When Chelsea left his side, Jonas glanced up to the New Mexico sky, wide and vast and endless. *I have really blown it. Why didn't I just ask Sabrina if Joe was mine?*

But Jonas knew why. At the time, he'd been terrified he'd spent over three years mooning after a woman he knew was way out of his league. She was wilder than him, she had more personality. She was a gypsy and Jonas was a heart surgeon—how was that going to work? A big part of his cowardice was not trusting the sexual attraction they shared. He'd never met a woman who could make him feel like a king and then a flunky at her feet. She'd turned him inside out from the day Jonas had met her. In fact, he remembered fainting. He'd thought he'd eaten something bad, but when he came to, she was standing over him in the living room. Jonas thought she was an angel staring down at him.

A very wild, very bad, superhot angel.

It had been all he could do not to look up her skirt.

Now my son is not wearing my name, the Callahan name. His birth certificate probably says Father Unknown on it, and—

"Damn it!" Jonas said, then cursed some more, electrifying the guests who'd ventured too close to the punch table.

This Father Unknown business was going to have to be fixed—pronto.

Chapter Two

"As far as I can see," Sam said the next day, when his five brothers had corralled Jonas in the upstairs library where they held their weekly meetings, "you have some 'splaining to do. Where the hell have you been for all these months?" Sam shook his head. "You are not the one who was supposed to go off on a major soul-seeking mission."

"That's right," Pete said. He lounged in one of the wingback leather chairs, comfortable in his position as the first-married of the Callahan clan. "I always felt you scoffed at those of us who were less settled than you. You've always been so...well, *stodgy* is the word that comes to mind."

"Not too stodgy to fall for a gypsy," Creed said gleefully. "Remember when Sabrina was in her Madame Vivant days?" He shook his head with a grin and held up a cut crystal glass. "Here's to the joy of watching big bro go down like a sack of bricks."

"That's not fair," Jonas protested. "The whole Madame Vivant escapade is exactly what threw me. None of us knew at the time that she and Seton were Corinne Abernathy's nieces. It felt like some bell-wearing, exotic shyster had been let into our home by our fey little Aunt Fiona."

"Speaking of, we still have no coordinates on Fiona's whereabouts," Judah pointed out. He shrugged. "I guess she'll show herself when she wants to tip her hand."

Judah didn't seem too worried. As the father of twins, he had plenty of other things on his mind.

"I tried my best to find her and Burke," Jonas said, feeling defensive as he glared around at his brothers. "You have to understand, Fiona is not an easy woman to outthink."

"That's for certain." Rafe, the father of triplets with Judge Julie Jenkins, looked smug as he leaned against the fireplace. "And you were probably not the scout to send after her, bro. Not that we had much choice in electing you, as I recall. One day you were at Sam's first wedding, and then poof! You took a look at Sabrina's belly and off you went. It was an amazing thing to watch the studious, life-by-numbers-and-books guy go off on a major toot."

Jonas wasn't certain he felt a lot of sympathy in the room. Some gentle ribbing, perhaps, and maybe even a bit of *pull-your-head-out-bro!* He bristled. "Any one of you would have thought the same thing I did if the woman you loved was in a family way and hadn't told you. What was I supposed to think?"

"I don't know," Sam said. He was enjoying his newfound happiness with his wife, Seton, and their quadruplets. Jonas was still shocked that his younger brother had married before him. That was really almost the sole reason he'd brought Chelsea home with him. He didn't want to be poor Uncle Jonas, the doddering leftover to his many nieces and so far only nephew.

"Now that you've admitted Sabrina is the woman you love, what are you going to do about Chelsea?" Sam asked.

His brothers gazed at him silently. Jonas's heart pounded a ridiculous tattoo that a cardiac guy like him knew meant his body was in fight-or-flight mode. *Blast.* "Let's not go getting crazy here." He gulped his whiskey and looked at them mutinously. "I have not yet asked Sabrina if that is my child, and you don't know for certain, either, do you?"

They shrugged to a man. Either they weren't going to enlighten him, or they didn't know.

"Second, do you realize I was thirty-three when I first met her? I'm now going on nearly thirty-damn-seven. How long was I supposed to wait on her?" He sent a mulish glare around the room, pinpointing each brother. "Look, the common theory is that if a man isn't married by thirty-five, there's something wrong with him. I was beginning to wonder about myself!"

"We all were," Creed said easily. "You're not the quickest runner in the field, bro."

Jonas ignored that. "How long was I supposed to hope that she'd crook her little finger and let me know she felt the same way about me as I did about her?" He shook his head. "All you guys went whango-bango! off the market. You jumped into sacks like you were potatoes, and suddenly started sprouting spuds all over the place. Me, I like to be a bit more measured about things."

"And yet what about little Spud Joe?" Judah asked

dryly. "Seems when you were doing your measuring, you forgot to measure for condoms."

Jonas leaned back in his chair, not about to dignify that with a return shot. How in the world could he have ended up with a baby who wasn't wearing his name?

It had happened because he couldn't stay away from her. Sabrina had made him crazy from the day he first saw her. He'd heard bells tinkling and stars falling to earth, and he'd never believed he could fall in love at first sight.

Yet I did.

"A FIANCÉE!" SABRINA changed into worn gray warm-ups and flopped onto the bed. "Of all the souvenirs I thought Jonas might bring home, a fiancée was not one of them."

Aunt Corinne shook her head. She sat in the white wicker rocker in Sabrina's upstairs room, looking as unhappy as Sabrina felt. "That was a shocker, I'll freely admit."

"I should never have come back to Diablo."

Corinne sighed. "Selfishly, perhaps, I like having you here. And while it will be awkward running into Jonas and Chelsea occasionally, you really won't see them that often."

Sabrina thought that unlikely. This was Diablo; what wasn't seen was talked about constantly. "We all live in each other's business here, Aunt Corinne, you know that. The thing is, I really like Chelsea, so I can't muster up any jealousy or bad feelings toward her. She seemed kind and interested and…" Sabrina frowned, hunting for the word she wanted. "She seemed like she wasn't in love with Jonas, actually."

"I picked up on that myself," Corinne said cheerfully. "Maybe this engagement isn't set in stone."

It was wrong to hope for Jonas's relationship to fall apart just because Sabrina had had a baby by him. "We're all adults. We can do the right thing for Joe without hoping for other people's unhappiness." Still, her aunt Corinne was right: Jonas and Chelsea hadn't seemed that gaga over one another. More like "just friends."

"Oh, I don't want them to be unhappy," Corinne said. "It just wouldn't bother me if the engagement got called off."

Sabrina rolled over to send her a pointed stare. "Aunt Corinne, you are not to meddle in any way."

Corinne's eyes sparkled behind her polka-dotted glasses. "I wouldn't think of such a thing!"

"And you are not to set the Books'n'Bingo Society, nor anyone else, to interfering with Jonas's choice," Sabrina said.

Corinne smiled fondly at her niece. "Well, I can't promise not to hope that all of you get your heads straight on what needs to happen. I believe in true love, after all."

Sabrina decided her aunt wasn't planning to do anything nefarious. "It's up to Jonas to be happy with his choice, so if he's happy, then I'm happy for him."

"That's very mature of you, dear. I commend you." Corinne looked down into Joe's portable crib, where he was sound asleep, undisturbed by their conversation. "A busy time of being passed around by half of Diablo yesterday has tuckered our little man out still. I should let the two of you rest."

Suddenly, Sabrina felt tired herself. "Good night, Aunt Corinne. Thanks for everything." She settled her head on her pillow and smiled at her aunt. "It's all going to work out. I have a feeling about these things."

"So do I," Corinne said. "Good night, Sabrina."

Sabrina closed her eyes, only to start thinking about Jonas. How handsome he'd looked at the wedding! Better than she'd remembered, which was hard to top. The last time she'd seen him had been at Seton's first wedding.

Several months in Ireland had done nothing but improve him in some way she couldn't quite put her finger on. He seemed more mysterious, somehow more wise.

Definitely more hunk-hot in the way that only Jonas was to her.

Pooh. I'm not going to think about him anymore. Obviously, what we had wasn't all that special if he's put a ring on another woman's hand.

In fact, he's not hot at all. He's cold.

SABRINA WAS SHOCKED when she ran into Jonas bright and early Monday morning while taking Joe to the pediatrician. "Hi, Jonas," she said, walking past him as nonchalantly as possible. She'd wondered over and over what he thought about her baby—and when she should tell him the truth about little Joe.

"Wait, Sabrina." He caught up with her, matching her stride. "Can I carry something for you? You look pretty loaded down."

She had Joe's diaper bag, her purse and Joe. "No, thanks. I carry this all the time by myself."

"Well, it's too much gear for a petite thing like you. Let me take the baby," Jonas said, reaching for little Joe.

Sabrina gave him up reluctantly, watching Jonas's expression as he held his son. Interested faces peered out of shop windows, and their friends and neighbors who were walking along Diablo's sidewalks stopped to watch, even though they acted as if they weren't. Sabrina felt like a fish in an aquarium. Still, she waited as Jonas carefully studied little Joe.

Finally, Jonas glanced at her. "Is this my son, Sabrina?"

So this was how it was going to be. She hadn't planned to tell him on a beautiful, sunny May day in front of the hometown crowd, but he'd asked, and she wasn't going to prevaricate. "Yes. Joe is your son."

Jonas closed his eyes for a moment, pressed the baby close to his cheek. "What is his full name?"

"Jonas Cavanaugh McKinley. He was born on November 20."

He studied the baby, and Joe seemed to study him in return. "I assume my name is listed as the father on the birth certificate?"

"Yes, it is. Of course it is." Sabrina took Joe back, though Jonas seemed reluctant to part with his newfound son. "We have an appointment. I'm sorry."

She started walking at a brisk pace. Jonas kept up with her.

"What kind of appointment?"

"Six month checkup and shots." She didn't mean to

be curt, but this was so awkward, so unplanned, that Sabrina didn't know how to do anything else but put up her defenses.

"I feel I should be there."

She stopped and looked up at the tall, handsome man she'd once loved with all her heart. "Jonas, I appreciate that you're going to want to be active in Joe's life. But not today. I need…time."

He glowered. "I'm not trying to butt into your life, Sabrina. When Joe sees the doctor, I want to be there. Every time."

She sighed. "Fine. You can hold him when he cries."

"He won't cry," Jonas said. "He's a Callahan."

"He'll cry," Sabrina said, "because he's a baby. And it'll be loud and unpleasant, and you'll want to cry, too. But I can't take care of both of you, so you'll have to refrain."

He touched her arm to stop her dash toward the doctor's office door. "Sabrina, I can tell you're upset. I'm sorry. This isn't the way I wanted anything to turn out between us."

She didn't want pity. "Jonas, we never had a plan, so there's nothing to apologize for."

He nodded. "Still, I think you and I should talk."

"We will one day. I just don't know when." She stepped inside the office, glad that Jonas would have to stop talking to her about Joe now. This was harder than she'd thought it would be. She'd never envisioned him marrying someone else.

Joe squirmed in her arms, getting restless, and Sabrina searched for a bottle.

"Want me to hold him?"

"Sure." She handed Joe off to his father and kept rummaging until she found what she needed. "I suppose you'll want to feed him, too?"

"Can I?" Jonas's face lit up.

She sighed. "The nipple goes in his mouth."

"Sabrina," Jonas said, "I know how to feed an infant."

"Good. Here's the burp diaper." She flung a beribboned cloth over his shoulder. The six other mothers in the waiting room smiled at Jonas as he held the baby. He didn't notice the beams of approbation.

"Hi, Joe," he said to his son.

"I'm going to check in." Sabrina walked to the office window, signed in, then turned around, her heart catching as she looked across the room at Jonas.

This is what I came back to Diablo for.

Not that it was going to do her any good. "Jonas," she said, walking back over to sit beside him, "where's Chelsea?"

Jonas didn't take his eyes off his son. "She said now that we aren't getting married, she's going to try to find a job in Diablo."

"What?" Sabrina stared at him, astounded.

He shrugged. "She said she couldn't marry me now. That it would be a dumb thing to do, because we're just friends, anyway. She said I had a son I didn't know about, and I needed to get things straight in my life. I agreed with her."

Sabrina blinked. "I'm sorry. I didn't mean to come between you."

"You didn't. There was nothing between Chelsea and me to start with."

Sabrina thought that was unlikely, given Jonas's sex appeal. But she didn't ask any more questions, deciding that digging for more information wasn't really her place. "Do you want me to feed Joe now?"

"I think I've got the hang of it, thanks." Jonas stared down at his baby. "You just concentrate on picking out a date to marry me, Sabrina McKinley, because this boy's name isn't going to be Jonas Cavanaugh McKinley. It's going to be Jonas Cavanaugh Callahan, so we might as well get that understood between us right now."

Chapter Three

His brothers would probably say he was a dunderhead for blurting out his feelings—a bad proposal if there ever was one—in a pediatrician's office. And they'd be right. But holding little Joe sent such emotions washing over Jonas that it was all he could do not to throw Sabrina in his truck and drive off with the both of them. He could convince her on the road—he did his best work on the road.

That was something his brothers had never understood about him. They thought he was just an old fuddy-duddy, steadfast and boring Jonas the heart surgeon. He was that, in some ways, because he was the eldest and he'd felt a strong sense of being a role model when they were growing up. But there was nothing he loved more than to cut loose from the office and hit the road, experiencing the variety life had to offer.

"I can't marry you, Jonas," Sabrina said, interrupting his scattered thoughts. He was nervous—nerves akin to waiting for a bull to leave the chute—as he waited for her answer to the proposition he'd blurted.

"Sabrina," Jonas said, ignoring her statement. She was an adorably prickly little thing, but she didn't understand that a boy needed his father. A girl did, too, but Jonas had a boy, and right now he was dealing with the obvious. A girl could come later, if he played his cards right. "While you consider what I said, which is really not open to debate because Joe absolutely has to have my name, I want to show you what I just bought."

She looked at him suspiciously. "What?"

"It's not here. I'll have to drive you there to show you. Would you mind taking a two-day jaunt with me?"

"I'm not sure. Based on the marriage proposal you seem to be offering in a rather chauvinistic way, I don't know if I want to spend much time alone with you."

He nodded. "You owe it to yourself to find out. We belong together as a family, and that's the goal we need to work toward."

He'd hoped to see the light of joy in her eyes, but Sabrina's brows pulled farther together. "We don't have any goals, Jonas."

"I'm aiming to fix that." Jonas stood up with the baby when the nurse called little Joe's name. "What the three of us need is time away. See if you don't agree."

Sabrina followed him silently, which was unusual for her, because she was a firecracker and given to both opinions and the occasional explosion when put upon. He liked the fire in her. *Funny that I ever thought she was all wrong for me. It must have been the gypsy bells and the clairvoyant oogie-boogie that made me think she wouldn't be happy married to Steady Eddy.*

He could fix all that.

"You're crazy," Sabrina told him as they put Joe on the scales, and the nurse smiled.

"Big boy," she said, and Jonas smiled.

"Yes, ma'am. Just like his dad."

"Oh, brother," Sabrina said.

Jonas beamed hugely. Now *that* sounded more like the gypsy who'd rocked his world.

He was so glad to be with her.

He'd have to work on the relationship part. But he remembered how good "Yes, Jonas" sounded, and he was willing to try his darnedest.

IT TOOK TWO DAYS OF wondering how to politely do it, but Sabrina finally got up the courage to investigate her very attractive rival. "Excuse me," she said, walking up to the Diablo library desk with little Joe.

The redhead at the counter sent her a wide, welcoming grin. "I know you. You're Sabrina McKinley, and that's Joe. Hi, Joe," Chelsea said, giving his cheek a slight caress. "He sure is a happy baby."

Sabrina was warmed by Chelsea's Irish accent and the fact that the woman honestly seemed pleased to see little Joe. She couldn't pick up any animosity or jealousy from her, either. Sabrina's curiosity was killing her. Before she accepted Jonas's invitation to visit what he'd bought, she meant to speak with his supposed ex-fiancée.

Once burned, twice shy....

"Hi, Chelsea," she said. "You found a job so quickly."

"Yes." Chelsea smiled again. "I'm fortunate. Word got around that I was looking, and someone called me. I've got my passport, of course, and I applied for a visa. Then, one day, maybe a green card."

"That's a lot of plans," Sabrina said, holding Joe as he squirmed, trying to reach for a book. Chelsea handed him one, a children's picture book, and he instantly tried to gnaw on it.

"No, honey," Sabrina said absently, putting him into his stroller so he could "read" the book. "This is for higher education, not nutrition. You turn the page like this. See?"

Joe observed, but didn't quite have the motor skills to figure out page-turning. Still, he was happy to pat the page for a moment. "So," Sabrina said, "I guess what I really want to know is if you…if you're—"

"If Jonas and I are still engaged." Chelsea nodded. "No. We're not. It was Jonas's plan, to keep him from being embarrassed that he was the only brother without a woman. He was pretty devastated when he thought you'd gone to Washington and met another guy."

"Oh," Sabrina said. "That's not what happened at all."

"And any woman could have figured that out." She nodded again. "But Jonas was in full protective mode. I figured the two of you had to work things out eventually."

"So why did you come to Diablo?" Sabrina asked, wondering what Chelsea's angle was, if not marrying Jonas.

She began checking in some books that were in the bin. "I've been taking care of my mother for a few years. She's much better now. She told me to go see the world." Chelsea glanced at Sabrina. "Mom lives next door to Fiona, you know."

"I didn't know."

"Mom's supposed to be keeping an eye on Fiona and

Burke's place until they get back. Who knows when that will be?"

"They're elusive," Sabrina murmured. "So did you tell Jonas you wanted to see the world?"

"Mmm. And he said New Mexico was a great place to begin. That if I'd pretend to be his fiancée, he'd fly me over here and help me get started." The redhead grinned at her. "I want to do a lot of traveling, but I can tell Diablo is a great place to live. I may stay here for a while. I like family places."

"Diablo is certainly that."

Chelsea stopped checking in books for a moment to consider Sabrina. "You know, men think with their hearts more than we give them credit for. And Jonas really was freaked out that you were having another man's baby."

"It never occurred to me that he would think that," Sabrina said.

"There's the trouble," Chelsea said cheerfully, going back to her work. "We never know what they're thinking, and it's usually nothing that *we'd* think at all."

"Thanks, Chelsea," Sabrina said, feeling immensely relieved. "I really appreciate you telling me all this."

"Jonas can't be annoyed with me for telling you the truth, can he?" She winked at her. "Anyway, he's a nice guy and all, but I'm looking for adventure."

"You'll find it here." Sabrina handed the picture book back to Chelsea, and little Joe let out an indignant squawk. "Oh, Joe, honey…all right," she said, giving in. "I think he'd like a book to read, Chelsea." She found her library card and checked the book out, then gave it back to him.

Chelsea looked over the counter at Joe. "Maybe he's going to be book-smart like his dad."

Sabrina laughed. "Maybe he'll get some other kind of smarts from his mother, too."

"Goodbye, Sabrina. I'm sure I'll be seeing you around."

She nodded. "I hope so. Goodbye, Chelsea."

Sabrina went out, feeling much better now that she had some answers—and still not certain what to do about Jonas's invitation.

"So this is it," Jonas said proudly the next day, when he'd finally dragged a reluctant Sabrina and little Joe away from Rancho Diablo for what he called "new family togetherness."

Sabrina wasn't certain what she thought about "family togetherness" time with Jonas. After her chat with Chelsea, though, she'd decided to give it a shot. Something was bugging her, though she couldn't put her finger on it. The old "tickle" was back, warning her that something wasn't quite as it should be.

Jonas was handsome as ever, gorgeous, in fact, yet she couldn't allow herself to focus only on her emotions. But it was hard to forget what they'd shared, and how wonderful Jonas made her feel when she was in his arms. "What is it?" she asked, caution dampening her enthusiasm.

"This is Dark Diablo," Jonas said, parking his truck in front of a small, spare farmhouse set among hardy junipers and spiny cacti, and framed by dusky canyons and arroyos. "This is my new home."

Sabina blinked. "Home?"

"Yep." He came around to help her out of the truck, then took Joe from her arms when she'd released him from his car seat. "This is Daddy's new house, son. You get a swing set here, and a pony."

"Wait," Sabrina said, following them. "This isn't home. You live in Diablo, at Rancho Diablo."

"I've always wanted my own place. This is that place." Jonas glanced around, pride evident on his face. "It took me almost four years to finally pull the trigger and buy this from the owner, but I did it."

Sabrina looked around at the vast emptiness, her heart sinking. Of course, they were only a few miles from Rancho Diablo, but this wasn't home. Home was with the people she'd come to know and love. She didn't want Joe growing up alone.

She shivered. "There's nothing out here."

"I know. But I see cattle breeding and horses, and maybe something else. I'm not sure what." Jonas smiled at her. "I can tell you're not crazy about it."

"It doesn't matter how I feel," Sabrina said quickly. "It's your place. But it just seems so lonely."

"The previous owner was old. He'd sold off most of his equipment and buildings, intending to sell the ranch to a corporation, I think. But when I heard that we might lose Rancho Diablo, I began to think seriously about this place. I knew we could move our operations here, if we had to."

Sabrina nodded. "That makes sense."

"So now it's mine. Come on inside."

The small farmhouse, with its weather-beaten paint and dust-laden windows, was so different from the seven-chimneyed, English-style manor house at Rancho

Diablo. Sabrina walked into a wallpapered kitchen that was large and bright, if not updated. "Where does the water come from?"

"Here we're cistern. For the cattle, luckily, there's a couple of good creeks and streams you can't see from the house, but which I think I can run pipe to."

She kept walking around the house. "It feels like Auntie Em's home in *The Wizard of Oz*."

"I plan to build my own place one day. This isn't big enough for a family. And I like what I had growing up."

"Where are the closest neighbors?"

He looked at her. "I think there's some a few miles away. This is ten thousand acres, so it's pretty private."

"I'll say." She went up the staircase, finding three small bedrooms laid out at the top, with one bathroom in between. "All the bedrooms are upstairs."

"Yes." Jonas came to stand beside her, carrying little Joe. "Sabrina, everything can be changed."

She swallowed. "I've lived in a lot of places, Jonas, so I think I'm pretty good at adapting. But I suspect you're going to be very lonely out here. I know I would be."

He blinked. "Lonely? I was thinking how great the peace and quiet would be. I had five brothers growing up. Solitude sounds like heaven."

She shook her head. "I only had Seton."

Sabrina went back downstairs, and Jonas followed her.

"I don't want to be a wet blanket," she said, "so congratulations. I'm glad you got what you wanted."

His proud smile dimmed. "Thanks."

She nodded uncomfortably. "I guess we'd better head back. Thanks for showing me your new place."

Jonas looked at her for a long time before slowly nodding in turn. He led her to the truck, handed Joe back to her to put in his car seat, then drove away in silence.

Sabrina looked back at the small farmhouse set in the vast acreage, and wondered why Jonas wanted to be alone so badly.

"Jonas," she said slowly, "why do you want to run away from your family?"

"I don't."

She hesitated. "Are you sure? Because you couldn't have picked a more isolated place to live." She looked at him curiously.

He shrugged. "Maybe it's not for everyone. It's great for me, though. Nobody around for miles, until you get to the town of Tempest. I don't go there often. It's too much like Diablo. Full of well-meaning folk."

Intuition hit her. "Jonas, you sold your practice. You got a fake fiancée. You've bought a property where there's no one around to bother you." She gave him a steady stare. "You're hiding."

"Hiding?"

She nodded. "It's your typical pattern. You know what you need to do, but you stick your head in the sand instead."

"That's ridiculous," Jonas said. "It's a piece of land, Sabrina, not a crystal ball."

She wrinkled her nose at his retort and decided to ignore it. "Perhaps I'm trying to say that I suspect you still have a lot to figure out in your life, Jonas."

"I'm doing fine. And when you're not busy trying to make my life a piece of your investigative reporting, you'll probably notice that I'm doing very well, thanks."

"You are." Sabrina knew she was hitting very close to whatever was really motivating Jonas, or he wouldn't react so sorely. "But you'd do better if you'd finish what your brothers have started."

Jonas took a long time to answer. "Maybe," he said softly, "but I'm not going to."

Not surprised by his answer, Sabrina turned to look out the window as the dry, almost barren-looking land rushed past. "There's something bugging you at Rancho Diablo, or you wouldn't be trying to hole up out here."

"Nope."

"You thought I was pregnant by another man," Sabrina said with some heat, "though I can't imagine what that says about how you really see me—"

"I see that you're a little different from other women, Sabrina, which I happen to like. It scares me, but I do like it."

"When you're not scared."

"*Nervous* is a better word. Some people are afraid to try new foods. I'm not. You're a different kind of female than what we have on the ranch right now. But I need spice in my life, and you're the cayenne pepper in my chili." He ran a palm over Joe's small head, where he was strapped in his carrier between them. "And this is my tiny jalapeño on top," he said. "Good for me I've got the stomach for all this new fire."

Sabrina wasn't about to let Jonas pacify her with what he likely thought were compliments. "You went and found someone—"

"More calm, more sedate," Jonas supplied helpfully.

Sabrina was outraged. "Chelsea jumped on a plane with you to fake an engagement. How sedate is that?"

He laughed. "Okay."

"Anyway, don't get me off the subject. What I'm trying to point out is that you run off when you want to avoid things. Just like you ran off to Ireland." She glared at him. "How would you have felt if, upon seeing Chelsea, I'd jetted back to D.C.?"

"I'm glad you stayed. I'm hoping to talk you into living at Dark Diablo with me."

"If you don't put all your skeletons to rest, they'll pop back up. Contrary to me being the wild and unsettled one, you wear that badge, Doctor."

"Not me," Jonas said. "Surgeons do not have a wild bone in their body."

"Right," Sabrina said. "Anyway, that's what I think."

He sighed. "I won't deny all of what you say."

"Good." She popped the top off a bottle and began feeding the baby. "It's very important for little Joe to know that his father is a man of deep character, not given to wayfaring."

"Wayfaring." Jonas laughed. "Ha-ha-ha. I don't think I've wayfared in my life."

"Except to Ireland, and you brought back a pretty fancy souvenir."

"Okay," Jonas said again. "So what do you suggest?"

"That you do what you're meant to do."

He scratched under his hat, then shook his head. "What if I told you that the questions don't bother me as much as the answers might?"

"I would probably say the monster in the closet isn't usually what you think it is once you open the door."

"Ah-ha!" Jonas wagged a finger. "But sometimes it is."

"The good part is you'll be rattling those skeletons for little Joe's sake, and all your nieces and nephews, as well as your brothers. You want to be a hero for Joe, don't you?"

Jonas sighed. "I'd like to say not especially, but I don't think you'd believe me."

Sabrina smiled. "I probably wouldn't."

He glanced at her. "Would you be willing to be my shotgun rider if I start opening those doors?"

Sabrina looked into his navy eyes. "I'll ride shotgun."

"And then you'll marry me."

She blinked. "Was that a proposal or a typical Callahan pronouncement? I always thought if you ever asked, it would be a lot more romantic."

"Have I not asked you before? Because I have about a thousand times in my mind."

"You see, Joe," Sabrina said to the baby, who was contentedly sucking on his bottle and watching her face, "your father just delivered a half-baked proposal because he was afraid I might say no. Your dad protects himself."

"Not true," Jonas said. "I assume that a woman wants to marry the father of her child."

"I might marry you," Sabrina said, "but with a proposal like that, you can be certain you won't make it back into my bed."

"Oh," he said. "I better up my game."

"All of it, Doctor," Sabrina stated. "I hope you can."

"We'll see," Jonas said.

"So, BASICALLY," JONAS told Sam that night, "Sabrina hated Dark Diablo and didn't accept my proposal. My big moment and I came up zeroes."

"Not surprising," his brother mused. "You did kind of half bake the thing. Sabrina's right about that."

"Yeah." Jonas sat in the library drinking a whiskey with Sam, wondering how he'd ended up like this.

"The problem," Sam said, "is that you always underestimated Sabrina. She's way too good for you, for one thing."

"This is true," Jonas admitted. "She says I have to amp up my game, and I'm not sure how much amp I've got."

"You want her, don't you?"

"Hell, yes." Jonas stared at the whiskey in his glass as if it held answers. "But she's not a gentle and shy dove like your wife."

Sam hooted. "Seton is not gentle and shy. She's more like fireworks in my sky, trust me. Let's do a further checklist. Judge Julie is a smokin' pistol set to fire. Jackie was a nurse and keeps order like a general. Darla is a businesswoman, and there are days when I can hear the grocer grinding his teeth from the deals she makes him give her. Aberdeen may be a preacher, but she's got a soul of iron, don't let that sweet face kid you. Where are the retiring wallflowers in this family?"

"This is different," Jonas said.

"Only because it's happening to you this time, you big wienie," Sam shot back. "Believe me, we all suffered when we fell in love, though we mostly suffered because of our egos. You're just going to make more noise about it, I'm afraid. We'll have to resort to earplugs."

Jonas snorted. "Sabrina says I have to find myself first. She says I run away from what I don't want to deal with."

Sam snickered. "Guess she didn't have to be clairvoyant to know that."

Jonas looked at his youngest brother. "It's not true."

"Of course it's true. Every word. Did she set a goal for you, a dragon for you to conquer, in this quest for yourself?"

Jonas thought about it. "She says that until I've figured out the answers in our family, I likely won't be ready to make a good husband and life partner. Sabrina says that I've been avoiding my responsibility for years, and that it probably all goes back to the fact that I was the oldest. She says her hunch is that our parents leaving affected me the most. It's all a bunch of psychological nonsense, but I'm humoring her. It's best to let women think they're figuring us men out, you know."

Sam sighed. "That is not a good attitude to take."

Jonas was satisfied with his non-emotional approach to his chosen lady. "How would Sabrina know what I need to do to make myself into a good life partner?"

"Well, you ran off and got engaged to a woman you didn't love because the woman you did love was pregnant with your child. Call me crazy, but you may have some issues to iron out, bro."

He scowled. "Even if I did—and I'm not saying I have any issues at all—I wouldn't know where to start."

Sam raised his glass. "We did the spadework for you. All you have to do is put it all together."

Jonas stared at him. "Not that easy, when you consider that it's taken all five of you to get this far."

"Well," Sam said, easing back into the leather chair more comfortably, "if it's true what Seton discovered, and our parents are still alive, you have to find out where they are. And why they went away. They had to have left us for some real good reason."

"They went into witness protection because they're hiding from a cartel they turned over to the various authorities involved. You can't find someone in witness protection, no matter how much you might want to."

"Yeah." Sam scratched his chin. "But someone knows something."

Jonas shook his head. "That could only be Fiona—and she would absolutely never tell—only Chief Running Bear might know."

Sam nodded. "Bingo."

"But so what if we did find our parents? If they wanted us to locate them, they would have given us a signal, a clue." Jonas wasn't sure this particular holy grail had a desirable outcome. "The bad guys, whoever they are, might find our parents, too, then. I don't think it's worth taking a risk."

"You make several good points. Did I tell you, by the way, that Sheriff Cartwright had to release the guy he'd arrested? The one who was living in the canyons, and who rigged Seton's laptop?"

"No," Jonas said slowly. "Why did they release him?"

"He got bail from someone. A cash bond. And there wasn't enough to hold him on."

Jonas remembered how much trouble the rat had managed to cause over the years for their family. He'd bided his time, waiting for Jeremiah and Molly Callahan to contact the children they'd left behind. "It's not safe to find them, Sam. We could lead danger right to their door."

"I think you may be right." Sam looked at his boots, then crooked a brow at his brother. "So you'll just have to tell Sabrina you're probably never going to find yourself."

"Maybe." Jonas thought it was a real possibility, anyway. He didn't have the fire in his belly to know more than he did. Were they really alive?

Maybe finding out more about myself isn't what I need to quit avoiding the big issues. I'm a surgeon, for God's sake. I made life-changing, lifesaving decisions, every day of my life. What the hell am I afraid of?

It was simple enough. He was afraid of being abandoned, left behind once again. What had happened to drive his parents away?

As a child, he'd figured he must have done something bad. Something horrible, to make his parents leave and go away forever. God wouldn't take parents away from a boy who was good.

It had been years before Jonas had understood he had done nothing wrong, that death had come unnaturally early to his parents. The learning process of grief and abandonment might have even stirred his desire to be a saver of lives.

But the habit of backing away from emotional moments stayed with him. He didn't want to disappoint anyone, hurt anyone, because he or she might leave.

So much easier just to avoid the big issues.

"I don't know what I'm going to do about Sabrina," he said. "She doesn't think I've got the ability to stick with it for the long haul."

"She has a right to be a little antsy," Sam said. "You pretty much shocked the entire town when you brought Chelsea home. And now what are you going to do with her?"

"Nothing. She seems happy working at the library and doing her own thing. She's making lots of friends. I told her I'd send her back to Ireland anytime she wanted to go, on my nickel, but she said she's having a blast." Jonas shrugged. "She and Sabrina seem to get along, too. So I guess I just don't think about her much."

"You realize that, out of all of us, you made the biggest boneheaded error of courtship? Bringing another woman home," Sam said, disgusted. "I didn't dare even look at another woman when I was trying to catch Seton. I was too afraid she'd head back to Washington. I'm kind of surprised Sabrina hasn't, actually."

Jonas sat straight up. "She wouldn't."

"She might." His brother shrugged. "She still keeps an apartment there, and you're the world's slowest Romeo. She may get impatient with you. I would." He drank his whiskey and closed his eyes with sheer contentment. "I think she's spotted you a couple of forgiveness points because everyone recognizes you're a little impaired in the love arena, but I wouldn't push my luck."

Jonas felt himself go pale. Sabrina was a traveler,

and fiercely independent. She did have a job in D.C., but she was on maternity leave.

He had to make like a retrofitted Romeo—fast.

"Anyway," Sam continued, "Sabrina's right. You do have a pattern. You would never have bought Dark Diablo if you weren't looking to get away from all of us. It's called shirking your responsibilities. How did Sabrina know you'd never change?"

Jonas gawked at his brother, wondering when having a dream had become shirking his responsibilities. "You know, I'm not the bad guy you paint me as."

"Nothing bad about being terminally uncommitted and unable to participate in a family." He shrugged. "We got used to it after you went off to college, then med school, then Dallas. But as far as a woman goes, Sabrina in particular, does she have any reason to expect much from you?"

Jonas didn't reply. What the hell did his brothers know about anything, anyway?

He could be Dr. Commitment.

He could fix everything.

"I THINK MATTERS ARE pretty much as you'd want them to be, Fiona," Chelsea said on the phone that evening as she relaxed in the Callahan guesthouse. It was comfortable here. The Callahans were nice, and they never bothered her, just seemed determined that she eat with whatever Callahan brother's family had an extra seat that night. Altogether, being here was an enjoyable adventure, and the experience would give her a lot of material for the next mystery she was writing. "Jonas has a new baby—"

"A baby!" Fiona's voice was like an explosion in her ear.

"Yes. His name is Joe. Sabrina's the mother—"

"Sabrina McKinley!" Fiona chortled. "That is going to be one wily child. I wonder which parent he'll be most like? Jonas is slow and studious, and Sabrina is quick-witted and adventurous."

"He looks like Jonas," Chelsea said thoughtfully, "but I do think he has some of his mom's mannerisms. Sometimes when he sits in his carrier looking out at the world, I could swear he knows exactly what's going on."

"Tell me more," Fiona said.

"Well, there was some guy here who apparently hacked into Seton's computer in his effort to find your sister and her husband—"

"What?" Fiona's voice over the phone sounded strained. "They caught him?"

"I heard they did." It was hard to listen in on conversations around the ranch and not ask questions. Chelsea tried not to arouse suspicions. The last thing she wanted anyone to know was that Fiona had put her up to coming over with Jonas to "report" on the family. When he had proposed, it had seemed to Fiona like a golden opportunity, and she'd hatched this plan. Chelsea had been fine with it, excited to come to America, but she'd quickly figured out there were a lot of deep currents under the seemingly placid Callahan waters. "They had to release him, though."

"That worries me."

"It was strange, because the guy had been living in the canyons for years, biding his time. Sort of a secret cell, waiting for something to come to light."

"Hmm. I don't like the sound of this. Chelsea, are you all right in Diablo, or do you want to come home?"

"I'll be fine for another week or so, I think." It really was pretty in Diablo, so different from Ireland. Her mother was in good hands at the moment, so an adventure was probably best for all of them.

"Thanks. I'll talk to Burke and see what he thinks we should do. Call me soon, all right?"

"I will." Chelsea hung up the phone and looked out the window, where she could see Sabrina and Jonas with little Joe. She smiled at the picture the three of them made. Never had she seen a man more gaga for a woman than Jonas. He really had been fooling himself about not marrying Sabrina.

I'd like having a man so crazy about me. The problem is, I'm too picky for my own good.

"I CAN'T DO IT," JONAS told Sabrina as they took a stroll around the ranch that night. Little Joe dozed in Jonas's arms. "I can't find myself. You'll have to choose some other Herculean task for me to perform."

Sabrina stared at the man who'd fathered her child, and shook her head. "What spooked you?"

"I'm not sure. It was a combination of things. You'll have to choose a different test."

Sabrina watched the moon glowing in the New Mexico sky, and thought it was the most beautiful thing she'd ever seen besides little Joe. "It's not a test, Jonas. It's just giving you time to figure out what you really want in life. And you can't do that until you know what happened in your past. I think the past determines the future." She reached up to run her hand across his

cheek. "When I first met you, your aunt had hired me
to tell you a yarn. I did that, only because I knew Fiona
had her heart in the right place, that she was trying to
help you Callahans, and not hurt you. I just don't want
you to ever regret that you married a woman who was
out to trick you. Remember when I told you that the
ranch was in trouble?"

"Yes," Jonas said, "and it was."

"Well, that's the point. It still is."

He rubbed his chin. "Just from a different source."

"Exactly." She knew the sheriff had released the
man Sam had caught snooping around Rancho Diablo.
And why wouldn't the spy go right back to doing what
he'd been doing—trying to find their parents? After all,
that's what he'd been hired and trained to do. "Maybe
you should talk to him again."

"I don't think so. He's not going to give up any
more information. Anyway, you're going about this all
wrong. You should marry me, and then let me solve all
these issues as they become solvable."

"It's not that I don't want to," Sabrina said. "But you
have a lot to do. You don't need to be sidetracked right
now."

"There are more important things in life than worrying about the ranch, or about the past. Like watching
little Joe pull himself up today. I'd rather focus on the
good things."

"I know," Sabrina said, "but every marriage has
rough patches. Take care of this rough patch first.
You'll thank me later."

"I don't know," Jonas said. "I feel strangely compelled to get into bed with you instead of playing Sherlock Holmes."

Sabrina smiled. "I never said you couldn't seduce me, cowboy."

Jonas's eyebrows shot up. "You didn't?"

She shook her head slowly. "No, but maybe I should. You'll work harder."

"I was always the guy who worked best with incentives," Jonas said, pulling her close with his free arm. "Try me with the carrot-and-stick approach and see what happens, beautiful."

"Jonas!" Sabrina giggled and put up no fight as they stepped through the door of the main house.

Five pairs of eyes stared at them.

"Hi, Jonas," Rafe said. "Did you forget it's time for the weekly meeting?"

"Uh…" Jonas carefully untangled himself from Sabrina and looked around at his brothers. "Can I skip this one?"

"Jonas," Sabrina said quickly, "you have your meeting. I'm going to go give Joe his bath. 'Bye, guys." She gathered the baby into her arms and stepped back into the night air, taking a deep breath as she went.

It had been a long time since Jonas had held her. She couldn't wait to get her hands on him.

Yet rushing things wouldn't help anything.

She drove to Corinne's and went up the stairs to draw a nice bath for Joe. The house was dark and empty, and Sabrina wondered where her aunt was. She set Joe in the tub, washing him with a mild, lavender-scented shampoo. He splashed in the water, delighted with this playtime.

She didn't want to rush Jonas, but moments like these were so sweet they were meant to be shared with the father of her child. He'd lost six months of Joe's babyhood.

It would be easy to accept Jonas's proposal. But if she hadn't had Joe, maybe Jonas would have married Chelsea, or some other woman. What did marriage mean to Jonas? Partnership? Companionship?

Sabrina wasn't certain.

For her, it had to be true love. That's all she planned to say yes to—true love, the real deal.

"Or it's just going to be me and you, babe," she told little Joe, rinsing his hair carefully. "And we're a pretty good team, anyway."

Joe looked up at her and splashed the water again. Droplets flew, and Sabrina smiled. He was such a good baby, such a sweetheart. Being a mother was the best part of her life now, even though she'd never imagined how much having a child would mean to her. Motherhood had changed her in so many wonderful ways.

Being a father was going to change Jonas, too. It already had. She could feel him yearning to be with his son, so much so that she wondered if his feelings for her really were all about her being the mother of his child.

Only time would tell. Going slowly would give them both time to be sure, especially Jonas. If she never got to share parenthood with Jonas, that was the way it would have to be.

Life wasn't always perfect, even if she wished it so.

Chapter Four

One week after Jonas had nearly managed to get Sabrina into bed with him—almost!—he sat in the tearoom and bookstore of the Books'n'Bingo Society shop, staring at the three women who were determined to buttonhole him into civic responsibility.

Nadine Waters, Corinne Abernathy and Mavis Night wore smiles on their small, doughy faces that he just didn't trust. He sipped the tea they'd offered him, and waited for the zinger.

It came with typical directness.

"As you know, Jonas, your aunt Fiona was president of our society for many years. In her absence, I've taken over the reins as interim president. However," Corinne said, stopping for dramatic effect, "we think you should pick up where your aunt left off."

Jonas set down his teacup. "Ladies, I don't know the first thing about what this Society does. Nor do I have my aunt's finesse in whatever it was she did, which mainly appeared to be—" He started to say "being a busybody," but stopped himself.

"Running this town," Nadine said, finishing his sentence. "And an admirable job she did of it, too. How Diablo misses Fiona's sure-handed—"

"Interference," Jonas said, not realizing he'd spoken aloud.

"Yes," Mavis said. "There have been times when interference was called for. We could always count on Fiona to have the guts to make the calls that needed to be made, and to take responsibility for the issues that count most to this town."

"Damn it!" There was that responsibility word again. Why was everyone determined that he was Mr. Fix-It? "I mean, darn it," Jonas amended, and the ladies' feathers seemed a bit less ruffled. "While I appreciate your generous offer—it's quite humbling—I am just not your man."

They looked at him, downcast.

"Well, I'm not." Jonas met each gaze with as much diplomatic aplomb as he could muster. "I'm no good at busybodying—let's call a duck a duck here. That's what Fiona did. We all jumped to her puppet strings. But I'd make the world's worst puppeteer."

"You'd be an excellent ventriloquist," Nadine said dryly. "A lot of yakking is coming from your mouth right now, Jonas."

Their expressions seemed to say, *Shame on you for shirking your duty!*

Jonas sighed. "Really, ladies, I've got my hands full. I've bought a new ranch—"

"This is your home, whether you ever want to face that or not," Mavis said. Her silver hair shone in the soft light of the tearoom. "We understand you wanting to separate yourself from your brothers and stake your own claim, but Diablo is where your heart is, Jonas. Even if Fiona did say you had wandering feet."

He frowned. "We all did."

Corinne shook her head. "No, Fiona specifically said you were the one who ran from home the minute you could, but unlike most wayward sons, you stayed gone. The only reason you're here now is probably Sabrina."

He brushed off his hat. They were right, blast their bright eyes and busy minds! If Sabrina wasn't here, he'd be at Dark Diablo right now.

But he'd never considered himself a wanderer. "You know, I'd built a very successful practice in Dallas."

"We know." Nadine nodded. "And you can do that here."

He stared, the notion crashing in on him like unwelcome waves. "Here? I don't want… That is to say—"

"We know," Mavis said. "You don't want to live here. You don't want to take care of the many elderly folk in this town who have tickers that need help just as much as those in the big city. Folks who helped raise you and kept an eye on you since you were in diapers."

The guilt trip. It was a skillful ploy when used by the right people, and these three were pros. "I never thought about opening a practice here."

"We know." Corinne blinked at him. "We think taking this position as president would be a first step in getting your priorities straight."

Mavis nodded. "Civic duty is a sign of maturity and commitment to community."

Jonas flattened his mouth. In their minds, this position would begin to solder him to the town and community. But that wasn't going to help him get his life back on track. Still, a little glad-handing and tea-sipping wouldn't kill him.

"All right," he said. "I'll do it."

Corinne clapped her hands. "I told you he would!"

Mavis sniffed. "Congratulations, president of the Books'n'Bingo Society and interim mayor of Diablo."

"Wait," Jonas said. "You said nothing about a mayorship."

"Yeah, but it's past time we had one," Nadine said. "We appoint you until you can be duly elected."

"I don't want—"

"Civic duty," Corinne said.

Jonas sighed. "Fine. Do you want me to watch the jail or build on to the elementary school or perform any other civic thing while I'm here?"

The ladies smiled at him with approval. "You just help us get Diablo on the map, and you can do anything you want."

Jonas scowled. He had a new baby to take care of and parents to find. A ranch to get off the ground. Somehow these ladies had caught him in their cookie-baited trap.

Unfortunately, he did love cookies—and these dear friends of Fiona's were bakers *par excellence*.

THE MAN WHO WALKED into the library didn't look like a typical Diablo resident, but Chelsea couldn't place why she thought that. "Can I help you?" she asked.

"It just so happens you can, Red," he replied, and Chelsea frowned. Jonas called her Red. He was a friend. From anyone else, it felt too familiar. "Do you know the Callahans?"

Chelsea turned her attention to some books that needed to be checked in. "Everyone does."

She gave the man a covert glance. His sandy-colored hair was windblown. His blue jeans looked new but his shirt had seen better days. He was roughly handsome—not quite as gorgeous as the Callahan brothers, but not average, either—and he was built strong and wiry.

He grinned at her. "Like what you see?"

"I'm wondering why I haven't seen you before."

"Well, maybe," he said with a voice that sounded slightly demeaning, "because you're new around here yourself."

She frowned. "And how would you know that?"

"Rumor has it that you're Jonas Callahan's fiancée. Or were, until he got back together with his old flame."

Her frown deepened. "Jonas and I are friends. Sabrina and I are friends. You, however, are not a friend, and are obviously a very nosey person. If I can't help you with a book, I'll have to get back to my job."

The man laughed. "My name's Sonny Baker."

"I didn't ask."

He leaned on the counter. "You're a tough customer, aren't you?"

"You haven't got anything I'm interested in buying."

He laughed again. "Look, take it easy on the new guy, will you? I saw you at Banger's the other day, thought you looked like a nice girl, and asked a few questions about you." He smiled, trying to calm her suspicions. "Everybody says you're real sweet."

She didn't reply. He gave a put-upon sigh.

"I was going to ask you if I could buy you a drink when you get off work."

Chelsea folded her lips tighter and shook her head.

He edged closer. "So I heard you might even be

thinking about applying for a green card. That can take months, you know. Just applying for a renewal is six months. The whole process is long and expensive. Be much cheaper to get married."

Her gaze snapped to his. "I'm not interested in getting married."

"But you were, until you found out Jonas had a son."

She shrugged. "It all worked out for the best."

"Yeah." Sonny reached out and placed a hand over hers. She quickly snatched it away. "But what if I offered you the same deal? A friends-only wedding? One day at the altar so you could get your paperwork in order? And then a no-fault ninety days later?"

Chelsea stared into his golden eyes. "What is it you're after?"

"Just trying to help out a lady in need."

"I don't think so."

Sonny smiled. "Give me thirty days to prove to you that I'm a guy with a big heart."

She shook her head. "I'm planning to go back to Ireland soon," she said, not being truthful. She just wanted him to leave.

"Word is you like it here. That you've even been studying about the University of New Mexico online so you could get a student visa and be eligible to stay longer."

The frown jumped back onto Chelsea's face. "I can handle my own business, thanks. Now if you don't mind, I have patrons to check out."

She turned her back on him, and after a moment, heard his boots moving away from the counter. A shiver ran over her. There was something about the man that made her nervous. He knew too much about her—and he'd seemed very interested in the Callahans.

Chelsea told herself not to think about it. If she paid attention to every person in Diablo who knew too much about someone's business, she'd go mad. The town was a kettle of well-meaning interference, mostly in the good-natured spirit of community. He probably hadn't meant a thing by striking up a conversation—people did that all the time in Diablo, she'd noticed. And they were usually pretty well-versed about everyone's business, especially someone from a foreign country, as she was.

She'd never seen the man before—and likely wouldn't again. His marriage proposal had been a bit odd, but surely he'd been teasing.

Chelsea sighed. She took everything too seriously. As a mystery writer, she tended to look for MacGuffins and red herrings. No doubt the conversation had just been an idle getting-to-know-you on a sunny day in Diablo.

"JONAS," SABRINA SAID, as she tucked little Joe into the playpen in Rancho Diablo's main house, where Jonas was staying. "Can you babysit Joe tonight?"

"Of course I can watch my son!" Jonas frowned. "Why would you ask that?"

"Because I want to go out to dinner with Chelsea."

"I meant, why would you ask me if I would watch him? He's my son!" Jonas was pretty nettled about Sabrina assuming she had to ask.

"I just didn't know if you had a meeting or something."

He stared at her hungrily, wishing he had a meeting with his favorite redhead. "I don't. But even if I did, Joe could always go with me."

"I can see you holding your Books'n'Bingo Society meetings with Joe banging a spoon on the table." Sabrina smiled at him, and Jonas felt his heart flip over.

"Everybody knows what babies do. No one would care. Besides, this guy is special." He glanced at little Joe, warmed just by looking at him. "Why are you going to dinner with Chelsea?"

"She invited me. It sounded like fun. Is there a problem?"

"No," Jonas said. "Well, yes. Why aren't you going to dinner with me?"

"Because you never asked." Sabrina patted his shoulder, and Jonas scowled. Random pats were not what he wanted from his woman. The problem was, Sabrina didn't think she was his woman. She thought they were parents sharing diaper and handling duties for Joe.

"I suppose I hadn't thought to ask you out on a date," Jonas said, "but I did try to get you in bed the other day."

Sabrina looked at him, her lips barely curved in a smile. He could tell she wasn't offended that he desired her. He always had. Today she was wearing a white kind of peasant top, one of those full skirts she liked— he thought she'd called it a circle skirt but he didn't care for details other than length and tightness—and some pretty white sandals. He got warm staring at her, and wished she'd come sit in his lap and let him play with her while Joe slept.

"You did try to get me in bed, and I barely escaped.

It was fortunate that I did, because you have so many new duties these days. I wouldn't want to wear you out."

He tried not to grind his teeth. "I have a special Sabrina battery, thanks."

"Still," she said, "I think it would be a mistake for us to fall back into our old habit."

"But it was such a nice habit. I loved sneaking up the stairs to get in bed with you. I always knew you were at the top of the staircase, right up there—" he pointed to the second floor "—and the best part was, you were almost always naked. Did I ever tell you how much I liked you between my sheets?"

"About fifty times." Sabrina handed him Joe's bottle and a bag of stuff no baby should have to worry about. Jonas didn't remember Fiona or Burke ever hauling around a diaper bag for them. He was pretty certain he and his brothers had just learned to eat straight from the table. "Maybe we should try it again, just to make certain we still like it."

"No," Sabrina said, laughing. "Eventually, you'll figure out what you want in life. Good night, Jonas."

She went out the door, leaving him in a smoking mess of desire. The woman literally had no idea how she kept him in a perpetual state of— Well, longing was a candy-ass word when he really felt as if the top of his head was going to blow off if he didn't get to have her soon.

"She insists on romance, son," he told his slumbering boy. "And we never had that before, so it's a tough thing for me to factor into the equation."

Joe didn't care. He slept peacefully, unconcerned with his father's dilemma.

"Yeah, you just snooze away. Don't worry about your ol' pop. You were supposed to be my golden ticket to her heart." Jonas grinned at his son. Joe's skin was so soft, though he had Jonas's darker shading instead of his mother's porcelain-and-strawberry complexion.

Jonas glanced around the room, then settled into the big leather chair as he tried to decide what he wanted to do for the evening while the girls were out gabbing.

He wondered what they'd be gabbing about.

Probably him, and what an unromantic louse he was.

Jonas sniffed and hauled out his iPhone to tap in "romance."

This pulled up some unsavory things, so he cleared his phone in a hurry, with a guilty glance Joe's way. The internet wasn't going to be helpful, and his brothers were duds for advice, so he was going to have to think this through himself.

"It's very simple," he told Joe, who ignored him in favor of sucking a thumb in his sleep. "I want Sabrina. I know she loves me. At least she likes me a lot, enough to make you, so that gives me a leg up on the competition." That was a happy thought, so Jonas marked a "one" in the air with his finger. "Where we went wrong is that I thought she was pregnant with another man's child, and she thought I didn't love her." He frowned. He did love her. Why did women have to make things so hard? That was a point deduction in the relationship factor. He was back at zero. "Your mother wants to raise you and keep on doing her reporting. I already know that. I want to open a practice in Tempest, near Dark Diablo. Your mom didn't seem to cotton to Dark Diablo. And that's a problem."

Jonas frowned. That was another minus, so he was down one point, which didn't bode well for him mathematically, nor in a relationship.

Something had to give.

"Well, it's very simple. She's just going to have to understand that the man has rights here, Joe. A compromise is in order."

Sam walked in, overhearing the last bit of conversation. He glanced at Joe, who slept on, his world completely wrapped in lullabies. "Lonely, Jonas?"

"No. Just thinking out loud."

Sam set a six-pack of longnecks on the coffee table. "I heard the last bit. It didn't sound promising."

"I know," Jonas said darkly. "Thank you for noticing the obvious."

"I thought I raised you better than this." Sam pulled the tops off two longnecks and went to cut a lime. "Women do not compromise, bro. What did you not learn?"

"There has to be *some* compromise."

"No," Sam said, coming over to jam a lime slice in his brother's bottle, "*you* compromise. And then everyone is happy. That's how you win the woman. It's that simple. Don't try to make it hard, like you do everything else."

Jonas shook his head. "I'd have to give up Dark Diablo."

"Not necessarily. You just wouldn't live there full-time. We could use it as a base of operations." Sam waved a hand, as if he were a magician who could make all life's troubles disappear. "And you could still open your practice in Tempest. You know, commute."

"Yeah." Jonas wasn't certain he liked the way Sam was thinking, but he was beginning to see some dawning light.

"It'd be like having a lake house, only this would be a satellite ranch house."

"I didn't buy Dark Diablo for our vacation pleasure," Jonas said sourly. "I bought it to be my home."

"Sabrina's happy here. And you know, if I were you, and I had to choose between my wife and son being in D.C. or Diablo, I'd opt for Diablo in a heartbeat."

Jonas stared at his brother. "That's the second time you've brought up D.C. You know something."

Sam threw himself into the leather chair opposite Jonas's in the large den. "I know her unpaid maternity leave is up this month. I know her job is back there. She's staying here as long as she can. What else do I have to know? It's not rocket science."

Jonas blinked. "Holy smokes, for once you're making sense."

"No, for once you're listening." Sam grinned. "I think heart surgeons must have more trouble with the obvious than the rest of us. You want to make everything a complex puzzle."

Giving up his dream might mean keeping Sabrina and his son here. Jonas stared out the window, thinking he'd do anything to make that happen.

When Sabrina came to get Joe two hours later, Jonas had a plan. "How was dinner?"

She smiled. "It was fun to get out. Chelsea said to tell you hi."

Jonas looked at Sabrina. "Did you girls talk about what a great guy I am for those two hours?"

Sabrina picked up Joe and kissed his head. "You never came up at all."

Jonas didn't know what to think about that. "Shouldn't I have? I'm the only thing you two ladies have in common, aren't I?"

She laughed. "Jonas, you really don't understand women at all, do you?"

He was wading farther into deep water. Best to get back on ground he knew. "Sabrina, I'd like to take you out to dinner one night. Like, tomorrow night, maybe."

She smiled at him. "You're asking me out on our first date?"

Jonas felt some of the air and bravado go out of him. Why had he never asked her out before?

Because it was so much fun sleeping with her, and I was selfish.

"I can't tomorrow night, though, Jonas. Is there a chance you can watch Joe for me?"

Jonas perked up. "Of course I can! Would you stop asking? I'll always be available for my son!"

"Thanks." Sabrina gave him a smile that warmed his heart. "Jackie, Darla, Aberdeen, Julie and Seton are taking me out for a seven-month celebration."

"What are you celebrating?"

"Joe is officially seven months old tomorrow." Sabrina looked at him as if he was crazy. "Women keep up with these things."

Jonas frowned. His son wasn't getting any younger. By the time he got Sabrina to the altar, Joe was going to be wearing a cap and gown and graduating from

Diablo High. "Damn it, Sabrina! We've got to get Joe christened, at least."

Sabrina blinked. "I'm so sorry, Jonas. That happened months ago. I thought you knew."

Shock filled Jonas that he'd missed out on an important sacrament in his son's life. "How would I have known unless you told me?"

Sabrina felt awful. "Jonas, you were in Ireland. No one knew where you were or when you'd return. Of course I had Joe baptized! Sam is the godfather. Didn't *he* tell you?"

Sam had told him a lot of things, but not this. Jonas set his jaw. "There's a lot that people don't tell me around here."

Sabrina came over and touched his arm. "Joe's next sacrament is in second grade, and you'll be here for that."

She smiled, trying to make him feel better, but he didn't. "Sabrina, you have to marry me."

She sank into the leather chair where Sam had been sitting, and held Joe against her chest. "Speaking of impetuous proposals, Chelsea said a guy came into the library today and made some kind of proposal of marriage to her. Had you heard that?"

"No," Jonas said, trying not to sound as out of sorts as he felt. "And Chelsea's proposals are her business. Let's focus on the one I just offered you."

"Did you offer me one?" Sabrina looked at him. "I don't think I heard a proposal."

"It *was* a proposal."

"More like a command." Sabrina gazed at him with untroubled eyes.

"I don't want little Joe to be so old when we get married that he can stand in as my best man." Jonas couldn't understand why Sabrina didn't get the fact that he loved her, she loved him—didn't she?—and therefore marriage was a highly desirable outcome for both of them.

She shook her head. "For the moment, can we focus on Chelsea? I'm worried."

"I don't want to," he grumbled. "I want to focus on you." If life were fair, they'd be having this conversation in bed right now, two married people enjoying the fruits of finding unexpected love. *Instead, I'm over here and she's over there, and little Joe is probably the only thing keeping her in this room.*

"Why would a man suddenly walk into the library and know so much about Chelsea? He knew she was looking into staying here longer, and that she was in the process of getting permanent paperwork filed."

Sabrina finally had his attention. "That sounds like a stalker."

She nodded. "It bothered me. For the first time in months, I felt something."

He looked at her, waiting.

"I felt danger."

If Sabrina was getting a wave of clairvoyance, Jonas figured it was best to pay attention. Not that he understood anything outside the realm of allopathic medicine, but he was well aware Sabrina knew things other people didn't. It was something about her that had given him pause. Him, a man of science, who only acknowledged what his mind could verify.

Sabrina was all about the golden unknown.

Jonas hated the unknown. Concrete facts were so much easier to understand.

But he wasn't about to pass on a good hunch. "What kind of danger?"

She shook her head. "Something isn't right."

Jonas scrubbed at his chin. "Well, she sleeps in the guesthouse here. No one would dare come on the property."

"That mercenary did."

True. "All right. Maybe she should move into the main house," Jonas said.

Sabrina looked at him. "But you're staying in the main house."

"Yes," Jonas said airily. "Guess she'd have a built-in bodyguard."

Sabrina sniffed. "I don't know that I entirely like that idea."

"Don't know what else you want me to suggest, if you really think she might be in danger."

Sabrina pondered his words. "I'd feel dreadful if something happened to her."

"Tell me about it. Fiona would kill me."

"Jonas! That's terrible." Sabrina frowned. "It would bother you, too."

"I'm being very serious. Ask Chelsea if she'd feel safer in the main house." Jonas waved a hand magnanimously. "She can have your old room."

"Maybe *I* want my old room," Sabrina said slowly. "I'm sure Aunt Corinne would like a break from having a baby in her house."

"I don't think Corinne is all that worried about one

beautiful baby under her roof," Jonas said, reeling in more line.

Sabrina shot him a suspicious look. "Did you ever kiss Chelsea?"

"Nope," Jonas said. "Never crossed my mind, and I doubt hers, either."

Sabrina didn't seem mollified. "Maybe I will take my old room."

This was looking more promising. He'd have her close by all the time, and more chances for finagling a way into her bed—just like the old days. "Fine by me," Jonas said easily.

"Then it's settled." Sabrina stood and began packing little Joe into his carrier. "Chelsea and I will stay in the main house, and you'll stay in the guesthouse."

Jonas blinked. "That wasn't how I saw it."

She turned. "How did you see it?"

With you naked and waiting on me every night.

"I saw us living together like *Three's Company.* Remember that show on TV?"

Sabrina shook her head. "I never watched much TV. Sorry." She picked up the carrier and prepared to waltz back out of his life for the evening.

Jonas jumped to his feet. "So what about dinner the night after the Callahan women gabfest?"

She smiled up at him. "Maybe."

"Maybe?" She was killing him. Jonas was fully aware that his little woman was making him jump through hoops, and he could jump with the best of them. But right now he wanted something more than "maybe" from her.

He wanted a rock-solid yes.

"Yes," Sabrina said, and leaned up to give him a kiss on the lips that was a lot more than friendly.

Then she departed, leaving him transfixed. Glued to the floor.

"That's better," he said, watching her walk to her car. "I knew she couldn't resist me forever!"

Chapter Five

It was the hardest thing she'd ever done, but Sabrina planned on resisting Jonas for as long as it took—forever if necessary—until she knew for certain that he loved her for her and not just because she'd had his child.

"Although you are an angel baby," she told Joe, lifting him from his crib after she'd moved back into Jonas's old room upstairs at Rancho Diablo. Chelsea was down the hall, which was kind of nice—sisterly—and Jonas was in the guesthouse, though he was none too pleased about it.

Chivalry seemed to keep him from complaining, though he found every excuse he could to hang around the main house with her and Joe, whether snooping for cookies or just looking to hold his son. The situation was becoming a lot more cozy than Sabrina had planned. Their lives were starting to meld together in a family sort of way, which worried her.

It was never good to let Jonas get too comfortable, as she knew too well from before. What should have been just a sexual fling had become, for her, a real romance of the heart—*her* heart.

Not necessarily Jonas's, until little Joe.

"You're not going to be the holy grail your father tries to win, little one." She kissed Joe on his downy head and dressed him in some jean shorts that pulled on over his diaper, and a T-shirt that read *Cowboys Do It Better* across the back. Sam had left explicit instructions that this was the outfit of choice for today, but hadn't elaborated.

"Very rascally and altogether too Callahan, if you ask me. But since the T-shirt was a gift from Godfather Sam, I guess we'll go with it." Sabrina laughed at Joe as he lay on her bed, and snapped a photo with her phone. All he needed was a western hat and he'd look just like his dad.

Minus the T-shirt, of course. She couldn't envision Jonas ever wearing a T-shirt, much less one that had lettering.

Moments later, Jonas knocked on her door, poking his head around the corner. "Can I come in?"

"Yes." She picked up Joe and grabbed his diaper bag. "What are you wearing?"

Jonas stepped sheepishly into the room wearing a T-shirt that matched Joe's, the words *Cowboys Do It Better* stretched across his wide back in black letters. "This dumb thing is Sam's idea of a costume."

Sabrina smirked. "On Joe it makes me smile. On you, it seems like a raunchy pick-up line." He looked sexy in a bad-boy way, but she wasn't admitting it. No sense in puffing up his already humongous ego.

He shook his head. "I know. But all my brothers are wearing the same thing. We're apparently going to do an ad for Diablo, though I'm none too excited about the idea. I feel silly as hell."

"An ad for what?"

"You'd have to ask the Books'n'Bingo Society ladies." Jonas grimaced.

"Aren't you the president?"

"Apparently I'm more of a figurehead, a puppet president."

Sabrina laughed. "So what's the gimmick? A bachelor ball? A matchmaking festival?"

"I think we're supposed to advertise the family aspect of Diablo. Hopefully lure the right sort of community here."

"Wearing that?" Jonas's T-shirt was tight enough that it looked sprayed onto him. It was tucked into his worn jeans and topped by a big rodeo buckle.

The women were going to come running.

"But almost all the Callahans are already taken," Sabrina pointed out, heartily aware that there was a sixth—hers—still on the loose.

"The scheme, if I understand it, is that the six of us stand in a line, hats on, heads down. So the visual is of six hunky anonymous men, according to your aunt Corinne."

"I'll be speaking to her about this," Sabrina said, teasing. "So…where's the part of the ad that speaks to family?"

"Here," Jonas said, taking little Joe from her arms. "And you have him dressed exactly right for the occasion. You look just like dear old dad." He kissed his baby's head. "Sabrina, you are looking at the hottest men in Diablo County."

"I probably am," Sabrina said dryly. "Are all the Callahan babies going to be in the picture?"

"Nope. Just Joe. Because he's the big man on the ranch. Right, buddy? No? Your cousin Sam Bear is a big man, too? All right, he can hang with us for the photo shoot." Jonas headed down the stairs with his baby.

Shaking her head, Sabrina followed.

"You'll need the diaper bag."

"Thanks." He reached to take the blue-and-white-striped bag without hesitation, slinging it over his shoulder. "I'll have him back in a couple of hours. Unless you'd like to come watch?"

Sabrina hesitated. If she had good sense, she'd go protect her territory. There were plenty of single women in this town who thought nothing of throwing themselves at a Callahan. Lacey MacIntyre, who always wore sexy, tight dresses, and Wendy Collins, Diablo's much-married librarian, came to mind. Supposedly Wendy had had quite the thing for Jonas while Sabrina was in D.C. Once Wendy found out there was a baby on the way she'd headed for more eligible waters, but Seton had mentioned that they'd spent a lot of time together.

"Maybe I will," Sabrina said.

"Good." Jonas nodded. "You can beat the single ladies away from me."

Sabrina sighed, annoyed because Jonas had read her mind. "I doubt that will be necessary. You'll be holding Joe."

"Yeah." He kissed him on the head, and Joe flailed a fist in the air. "Ladies love a baby. That's what we're counting on in our ad."

"*We're* counting on?" Sabrina followed Jonas to his truck. "I thought this wasn't your idea."

"It wasn't," Jonas said. "But as president, I have to do what I can to support our town."

Sabrina got into the truck. "What about Dark Diablo?"

"I've got irons in the fire there, too, babe. Don't worry, I still have time for you." Jonas winked at her.

Sabrina buckled herself in. The man was entirely too full of himself. Cocky, self-assured, arrogant. Any adjective that went with those words, and perhaps even irresistible.

She stared out the window at the beauty of the New Mexico landscape as he drove them into town. "I missed it here."

"I did, too, while I was in Ireland. They say you can never go home, but I have." Jonas glanced at baby Joe, safely strapped into his car seat between them. "Home is where the heart is, after all, I guess."

"Jonas," Sabrina said, "if we hadn't had Joe, would you still—"

"Yes, Sabrina. I would still be here."

That wasn't what she'd been about to ask, and she had a feeling he knew it.

He reached over Joe to pat her knee. Sabrina shook her head and looked out the window again.

Joe, your father is being deliberately obtuse. Or maybe it comes naturally. At any rate, you'll probably get married before I will.

It wasn't the world's most cheering thought.

PRIVATELY, JONAS WAS embarrassed that he'd been roped into this ad. This was the kind of trap that Fiona would

have sprung on him, and the fact he'd been blindsided
by the BBS ladies (as he preferred to call them for effi-
ciency's sake) was not easy to accept. He was supposed
to be the new, big thinker in town. They'd elected him
president.

And yet he was wearing a pair of worn-in jeans and
a tight T-shirt, standing before two photographers in
Diablo's main gathering area, in front of the library.
About fifty of their friends stood around watching the
fun, but Jonas wasn't really having fun. His brothers,
on the other hand, were acting like hams. They ate up
the attention like it was blackberry pie. Jonas's attitude
darkened with each passing moment.

No one had told him that the Callahan men weren't
going to be facing the cameras.

The photos, every last one of them, were shot from
the back, the men's backsides the focus. As Jonas had
told Sabrina, the brothers did have their heads down,
looking over their shoulders with their faces covered
by their hats—because the layout was all about their
butts.

One of the photographers mentioned that man butt
was what impressed ladies most. Certainly the ladies
standing around seemed very pleased with the direction of the shoot.

Jonas felt like a Chippendales dancer.

And he'd invited Sabrina along. She was hearing all
the whistles from the crowd, and the photographer's instructions: *Flex those muscles, Jonas! Hold the baby a
little higher over your shoulder, Jonas!*

Only Joe's and Sam Bear's faces would be visible
in the photos. Corinne had said that was because the

babies were the only model-worthy participants, and the brothers had hooted her down.

Except Jonas. He'd glanced at Sabrina, noting that she didn't seem thrilled with his backside being Diablo's new ad.

As hard as it was to catch her—and playing it cool was taking every ounce of his willpower—he was never going to get her calmed down enough to marry him if she thought he was man candy. "Sorry about that," he said, walking over to hand Joe to her. "I had no idea what the shoot entailed."

"It's fine." She smiled at him, but it looked forced. "You do what you have to do. I've got to run, though. And don't forget, tonight you're babysitting while I go out with the Callahan ladies."

"Damn it, yes!" Jonas gulped, not meaning to snarl. The shoot had put his nose so out of joint he could barely hang on to his temper. "I mean, I've said before that I'm always available for being with my son, Sabrina."

"Hi, Jonas," Wendy Collins said, sashaying by. "*Great* shoot."

"Thanks, Wendy." He turned back to speak to Sabrina, but she'd headed off with Joe. He followed her. "And then we have a date the next night, right? Just the three of us?"

"Yes."

She didn't sound bowled over, or charmed by the idea of an evening with him. "Sabrina, thanks for coming today."

She turned to look at him. "I wouldn't have missed it."

He didn't know what to make of that. But she wasn't

the kind of woman to say what she didn't mean, so Jonas decided to let the whole thing slide. Maybe she was cool with it.

He hoped so.

But he had a funny feeling that date night might be his last chance to convince Sabrina that it was her, and only her, he'd ever wanted in his life. He could do this. If his five knuckleheaded brothers could win their women, he could do it, too.

In fact, he should be able to do it better and more easily than they had. He was the eldest. He had more life experience.

Who am I kidding? I'm so afraid Sabrina's never going to have me that I feel like I'm stepping around horse puckey. Piles of it. Eventually, I'm going to make a misstep, and the whole thing is going to be over. Pow! Just like that.

It's killing me.

JONAS HEARD ABOUT the Callahan ladies' night before Sabrina ever got to tell him because all of them came home singing, slightly off-key and very noisily. He shot to the window of the guesthouse to stare out.

Never had he known any of the Callahan brides to get even the slightest bit tipsy. Yet there they were, arms linked, walking down the drive together, having the time of their lives. His cell phone rang, and Jonas answered it.

"What the hell is that caterwauling?" Sam asked.

"It's your wife, and Joe's mom, and Jackie and Darla and even—holy smokes—even Judge Julie and cowboy preacher Aberdeen. This is indeed one for the books."

Jonas stared out as the women began doing some kind of line dance in the driveway. He had a perfect view of the fun because the moon was bright and some of the ranch's spotlights were pointed their way.

"Are they stewed?" Sam asked.

"I don't think stewed," Jonas said. "Maybe just loosened up enough to let their hair down."

"Hellfire," Sam said. "I wish I could see it, but I can't leave the quads."

"Don't worry. Imagine your wife acting like a coed, and you've got the visual." He thought it was great that Sabrina was right in the thick of things. In fact, he was getting horny just watching her have a wild-and-crazy moment with the girls.

Sam whistled. "I barely ever see Seton drink a beer."

"That's because you got her pregnant right off the bat." Jonas frowned. He'd gotten Sabrina pregnant pretty quick, too. "We'd best plan a vacation for these ladies, Sam."

"What do you mean?"

A bright idea bloomed inside Jonas's skull that he thought was good even for a thickheaded guy like him. "We've never taken a family vacation."

"Hell, no, we haven't. We have a ranch to run."

"Yeah." Jonas tugged at his ear. "But think how much fun it would be to take these ladies and babies to the beach. We can't do it now, the babies are mostly too young, but what if…what if we all went out to Dark Diablo and swam in the creek one weekend?"

"I'm with you on that." Sam sounded reflective. "Are they still dancing?"

"Yeah. They're bonding like mad. If we want to keep

our heads as the kings of our castles, we better ante up some relaxation and fun for these girls."

"Before you plan a vacation, bro, you'd best plan your wedding, don't you think?"

Jonas grunted. "Thanks for the reminder. I might have forgotten otherwise." He snapped off his phone and kept spying, enjoying the sight of the wives having a good time.

Wives and…Sabrina.

Damn it. It could not go on this way.

She was going to have to settle him down, the sooner the better. He could not go on being the wild one in their relationship. This was what he'd hoped to avoid—being the last lonely Callahan on the ranch.

Little Joe needed his mother and father to be a family.

Somehow, Jones had to convince her.

It wasn't going to be easy.

"THANKS FOR COMING," Jonas said the next day, eyeing the serenely smiling, wrinkled old Navajo. It never failed to amaze him how calm, how happy, the man seemed. Jonas felt as if he could look deep into Chief Running Bear's soul and see something he recognized. "I need to talk to someone about Aunt Fiona, and about our parents, and it's finally hit me that you're the one who might have the answers."

"Be careful of the questions you ask," Running Bear said. "Sometimes people don't really want the answers."

They squatted in the cave near the large rock. It had occurred to Jonas that this cave might not be simply

Fiona's storage facility. The existence of a mercenary hidden in the canyons had made him realize that things happened near Rancho Diablo that the Callahans weren't always aware of. "You know about the man who'd been living out here?"

Running Bear nodded. "Sonny Baker. He's been hanging around in town lately."

Jonas scratched at his day-old stubble. After watching the wives do their dance under the full moon last night, he'd been unable to sleep. The puzzle of how to convince Sabrina to marry him tore at him, kept him on edge and unable to relax. She'd said he needed to step up his game, and he'd asked her out on a date.

But he'd known that wasn't all she meant.

Jonas tried hard to think. "Why would he go into town, where we'll see him eventually, when he just got out of jail?"

Running Bear shrugged. "What's the harm for him to be in the open now? He thinks he has nothing to lose, and all to gain. And he wants you to know he's not afraid of you, so you'll be afraid of him."

Jonas considered that. Sonny could talk to townspeople, look through records freely. Folks might know he'd been arrested, but they didn't know why. Sheriff Cartwright wouldn't say anything about Seton's computer being hacked. And no one would know why it had been.

Jonas looked at Running Bear. "You know our parents are alive."

The old man's dark eyes met his with no expression.

"And you know where they are," Jonas stated. He

was guessing, but his heart hammered so hard he knew he'd hit on the truth.

"Be careful of the answers you seek," the chief reminded him.

"It's too late," he said. "I have to know. The truth will set us free, Chief."

"Maybe," Running Bear said. "The truth also imprisons sometimes."

"We've been in a prison since they left." Jonas thought about it, realized it was true. Fiona had done her best to protect her sister, Molly, and Jeremiah. She'd scattered the clues, stamped out any trail leading to their parents to protect them.

Yet they were still in danger. "If not Sonny, another will come," he mused.

"It doesn't matter. They will never be found," the old man stated.

Jonas didn't want to take the chance. "And if harm should come to one of the children because of whoever is seeking our parents?"

"Why?" Running Bear asked laconically. "The children know nothing, you know nothing." He eyed Jonas for a moment, seemed to come to a decision. "Still, there is a time to know. We will go for a ride. But bury your cell phone there first."

The chief indicated the large, flat rock where some silver bars and coins had been left, and under which some baby photos had been discovered many months ago. Reaching beneath the rock, Jonas found the hole it covered and tossed his cell phone in. The chief left the cave, and Jonas followed him into the New Mexico desert. They walked a long way, not speaking. Jonas didn't know where they were going, but if he didn't get back soon, he'd miss his night out with Sabrina. He had a funny feeling she was the kind of woman he didn't dare stand up.

Yet he had to know where Running Bear was leading him.

They must have walked two miles. Near the largest cactus Jonas had ever seen—he figured the thing could have put his eye out if he'd walked into it in the darkness—Running Bear raised his hand to his lips and whistled.

Two black mustangs appeared. *Diablos.*

"Damn," Jonas murmured. Neither he nor his brothers had ever been this close to one. The horses were hauntingly, achingly beautiful, wild-eyed and yet completely focused on the chief.

"We will go now," Running Bear told him, and swung up onto a mustang so smoothly that Jonas barely saw it happen. The Navajo grabbed the dark mane and the horse galloped away.

"Here goes nothing," Jonas said, and leaped onto the back of the other animal, which had let out a shrill whinny, almost a cry, when its comrade had raced off. "Let's go, brother," he told the mustang, grabbing its mane, and the horse fled from the canyon like a phantom, streaking after the chief.

Jonas held on for dear life. Wind whipped his face and pulled at his hair with urgent fingers. In the distance he could see the chief galloping hard, so Jonas squinted against the wind and murmured to the mustang.

It seemed they rode forever, until Jonas felt exhausted. The chief let the horses stop and drink occasionally, but they were used to long hauls between water so they never rested more than a few moments.

At least two hours beyond Rancho Diablo land, and so far from the canyons that Jonas and his brothers had never been there, the chief finally jumped down from his horse, which immediately went to a stream trickling past an outcropping. Jonas dismounted in turn. He was out of breath, but the chief seemed unfazed. It was a little disheartening that the older man was in much better physical shape than he was.

I've got to start lifting little Joe more. Maybe taking him on jogs in the stroller. He'd like that.

"Where are we?" Jonas asked.

"Near the New Mexico state line."

"We can't be!" He looked at the chief. "We would have had to pass Santa Fe."

"Hard to tell. Perhaps you don't read the sky for direction."

He hadn't been looking up; he'd been trying to stay on his fast-moving mount. Never in his life had he ridden so hard, so fast. "So now what?"

"We still have a little ways to go."

Jonas realized he wasn't going to make date night with Sabrina. The chief was on a mission, and Jonas felt as if tonight was a one-shot deal to find out the truth. He figured they'd traveled almost three hours, so whatever the chief had on his mind, it was going to be worth the ride.

"Let's do it," Jonas told him. They got back on their horses and they struck out.

This time, Jonas noticed they were headed north.

Chapter Six

A short time later Chief Running Bear finally stopped. He sat like a bronze statue, staring down into a green valley below. Jonas counted maybe eight wooden houses in a small enclave, surrounded by pines and other trees. Several small, dark-haired children played outside, and women chatted nearby. "Where are we?"

The chief didn't look at him. "This is our tribe."

Jonas stared down at the small village. "Your tribe?"

He nodded. "Our brothers and sisters who didn't settle in New Mexico with us."

Jonas wondered if the chief was going to visit them, but he sat still, not moving. After a moment, he dismounted and whispered in his horse's ear. Jonas dismounted, too, and the two horses lost themselves in the pines, where it was shaded and where he suspected they'd find water. He wondered if they'd be able to find them again when they were ready to leave, though Running Bear didn't seem worried. The old man sat down on the ground, and it crossed Jonas's mind that he might be going to nap. But he watched the activity of the village with interest, so Jonas did, too.

It was like another world. It *was* another world. He'd never seen people so cut off, although in some ways, the isolation reminded him of Rancho Diablo. But where his family ranch was surrounded by mesas and dry land, this area was green and peaceful. Not seeming to reach for the sky in a quest for rain, as Rancho Diablo did.

Jonas glanced at the chief. "Where do we go from here?"

Running Bear looked at him with gentle eyes. "This is the end of the journey."

It seemed like a long way to come just to sit and stare at a village. But Jonas knew that Running Bear had said all he was going to say.

The rest was up to him. Whatever the chief thought he should know, he expected him to figure it out on his own. Jonas took a deep breath, exhaling slowly. He crossed his legs and focused on the houses below. The chief had called their ride a journey. But a journey implied a destination, and Jonas didn't have one.

If he had a destination in his life, it was to end up at the altar with Sabrina and their son. He was in love with Sabrina. He had been for so long. Jonas breathed in through his nostrils, noticing out of the corner of his eye that Running Bear had pulled out a small pipe and lit it. He smoked like a contented chimney, and the fragrance wafted to Jonas, not entirely unpleasant on the fresh breeze. He breathed in again, and thought about Sabrina. What he loved about the red-haired gypsy was her independent spirit. She kept him on his toes, made his brain teem with thoughts of her. Around her he felt alive. When he'd learned that little Joe was his, he'd felt like a king.

Jonas was pretty sure Sabrina liked him, too. The

way she'd gotten a bit frosty over the photo shoot was cute. She hadn't wanted to admit it, but Jonas thought she'd had a slight bite from the jealousy bug. The memory brought a smile to his lips.

She made him smile often.

But if marrying Sabrina was the only journey he had in his life, why was he sitting here?

Another plume of pipe smoke came his way, and Jonas breathed it in. He felt himself growing relaxed, and maybe a little sleepy. Out of the corner of his eye, he noticed that the Diablos had returned, seemingly refreshed, and were standing near the chief. Their bodies were wet, so he knew they'd found a stream. Jonas felt himself relaxing more, and went back to thinking about his journey.

Sabrina had said that he needed to know his past before he could know his future. But he had no past; that was an established fact. None of them did. Whatever history the Callahans had was wrapped in mist, shrouded in smoke, never to be revealed or resolved.

Sabrina said the past determined the future. Maybe she was right. Who *was* he? Jonas's eyelids began to get heavier as the question ran through his brain. He was a Callahan, he was little Joe's father, he was a heart surgeon, he was a brother. He was half Irish, half Navajo.

He heard a movement, and realized Running Bear had motioned his horse over to him. Jonas's eyes snapped open. "Are we riding?"

Running Bear looked at him. "Are we?"

Jonas blinked. "I'm not setting the itinerary, am I?"

"You should. If you don't want to, then we will return."

Obviously, he'd missed a big detail. The chief expected something of him, but he didn't know what.

"Do you want to leave?" the old man asked.

Jonas glanced down at the village. It had to be getting close to the dinner hour because the men were returning home. The women went inside their cozy houses, calling for the children to take in their toys. They were all going into their homes for the night, where they would be together, families at peace.

His home was far away, and he was not at peace. But he knew there was something to learn here. "I'm not sure," he said.

"Be sure," the chief told him. "Leave no room for doubt in what you want to know."

What did that mean? Sabrina said he needed to know his past, but he didn't have one. Neither did his brothers, and they were all doing fine, despite their missing parents....

The truth hit him like a wall of falling bricks. He knew it even as Running Bear watched him curiously, preparing to swing up on his horse and ride if Jonas gave the signal.

Jonas stared down into the valley at the families and the homes, and suddenly he knew the piece he was missing was *here*.

He jumped to his feet. "I'm going down there," he said.

Running Bear shrugged. "Only go if you are ready."

Jonas's heart began to pound as it had never pounded in his life. "How will I know?"

"You will not ask, if you are ready." The chief tamped out his pipe, about to leave, but in that moment

Jonas felt that if he left this place he would never return, and he would never know.

He took off running for the village. No one, not even the devil himself, could have stopped him from ripping the veil of secrecy that had surrounded him and his brothers all their lives.

Chapter Seven

Jonas had stood her up. It wasn't like him to be unreliable, so not only was Sabrina disappointed, she was worried, too. He hadn't been seen since the day before yesterday, and his brothers said they weren't sure where he was, except that he might have driven out to Dark Diablo.

"Jonas can be dippy," Sam had said. "I wouldn't worry about it, Sabrina. Absentminded is his middle name."

Sam had smiled at her, and Sabrina had smiled back, not wanting to admit that Jonas had actually ditched her, something she was pretty certain he would never do. "Your father," she told baby Joe, "is not himself these days."

The baby tried to grab her hair, and settled for a hoop earring instead. "No, no," she told him, "you don't want that, honey. Let me get your giraffe."

They settled on a sofa in the living room. She loved it here. She hoped Joe could grow up at the ranch. There was a lot standing in the way of that, though. She and Jonas might not ever be able to make things work out. It felt as if they moved one step forward, then a whole mile backward. "He made such a big deal out of our date night, Joe. I just don't think he would have abandoned the idea without calling." She leaned back with the baby in her arms, comforted by his softness and warmth. "The thing that really bothers me is that ever since he found out you're his son, not one night has passed without him tucking you in." She smoothed her hand over the baby's head. "I think something's wrong."

But it wasn't her place to sound the alarm. The Callahans weren't worried, and they certainly knew Jonas better than she did.

I know he wouldn't go off and not call.

It was making her crazy. But then again, Jonas made her crazy in general. He'd gone to Ireland without telling her, and without communicating much with his brothers. At the time, he hadn't had a reason—at least not one he'd known about—to tell her he was leaving. But he had been calling her in Washington, D.C., as regular as clockwork—until he saw her stomach at Sam's first wedding.

Then he'd lit out.

So Jonas was capable of disappearing for months on end without feeling the need to tell anyone. And he did plan on living at Dark Diablo, away from his family. He'd lived in Dallas for years, barely coming home except at Christmas.

It was one of the reasons, Fiona had confessed, to wanting to start a competition among her nephews for the ranch. Everyone needed to settle down, and that included the brother who seemed the most stable on the surface, but was in truth the most commitment-phobic, light-footed of them all.

Fiona had known her boys well.

Sabrina shook her head. The whole ad for Diablo business had bothered her, too. Just when she'd thought she might be getting close to developing a relationship with Jonas, he'd starred in the family-fantastic, female-luring advertisement that the Books'n'Bingo Society had cooked up. He was the president, and had done nothing to curtail it. He'd even dragged little Joe into it.

She'd been miffed, no question. But she hadn't been about to show it.

"He might be every inch crazy, Joe, and I might have missed the warning signs." She kissed her baby on his head and closed her eyes. "At least I have you."

It was true. Joe was the light of her heart. Even if she never had Jonas to hold at night, to love, to live with as they grew older, she had this piece of him.

"You're my sweetheart," she told Joe, and rubbed his back. The baby laid his head against her throat and stuffed a fist in his mouth. Sabrina's eyelids began to feel heavy. She knew she needed to get up and put Joe in his bed, but right now, it felt so nice just to hold him. If she moved, he'd get restless, and it felt so good to have him all peaceful and relaxed in her arms.

She needed this right now.

"We'll just grab forty winks, Joe," she whispered, "and maybe your daddy will be back by the time our nap is over. We'll tell him if he ever scares us like this again, we'll know what to do about it."

Joe gave a small snuffle, and Sabrina dozed off, thinking about how much she wished Jonas was here so she could hold him and know he was safe.

"HOLY SMOKES," SAM SAID, gazing down at his oldest brother, "have you ever seen anything so useless? So ugly? So bone idle?"

Rafe shook his head. "Sleeping like a baby."

The five brothers stood around Jonas's bed in the main house guestroom, considering their brother with some amazement.

"He never sleeps in here," Pete said.

"He doesn't bathe much, either," Creed said. "If I didn't know better, I'd think he'd been riding for a couple of days. Someone open a window."

Judah grimaced. "Sabrina's going to kill him. She's been worried sick. She told Darla they had a date the other night. We were supposed to watch little Joe. But Jonas never showed."

"We all know about the infamous date," Sam said. "Believe me, it was all I could to keep Sabrina from calling Sheriff Cartwright. She was certain something had happened to our brother, the louse."

"And here he sleeps off a bender." Rafe leaned close to sniff him. "Doesn't smell like liquor, though."

"Smells a little smoky, but this room's been closed up awhile." Creed took a whiff, then backed away. "It's almost like he's been in some kind of trance. Like Rip Van Winkle."

"He's going to be in the super-doghouse with Sabrina." Pete looked chagrined for his brother. "I would never have stood Jackie up for a date."

"Pretty sure your path to the altar was anything but smooth, bro," Creed reminded him.

But it was true, Sam thought. Jonas, supposedly Steady Eddy Jonas, had just fallen very short of the ideal. Sam eyed his brother, who still wore his boots, had his belt and jeans on, and smelled like an unwashed horse. "Do we dump a bucket of icy water on him?"

"It's his life," Rafe said. "We don't know what demons are after him. I vote we let him sleep."

"Demons, hell," Sam said. "There's going to be fireworks like this ranch has never seen when Sabrina finds out he's been here all along."

"Someone has to tell her," Creed said.

Sam sighed. "I'll do it. Someone prepare me a tonic for afterward. I'm probably going to need it."

They heard the sound of the kitchen door opening and closing. The brothers glanced at one another.

"Fingers crossed it's not her," Pete said.

Footsteps sounded on the stairs, and then on the landing. Sabrina looked around the corner, with Joe in her arms, and Sam's heart jumped a foot.

"Is the meeting in here tonight?" she asked. Then her gaze landed on the bed. "Jonas!"

The brothers parted to let her through as they stood around the slumbering man. She looked at him, then glanced at them, knowing something was very different—wrong, even—about Jonas.

"Is he all right?" she demanded fearfully.

"Now, calm down, Sabrina," Sam said, trying to sound soothing. He realized he'd overstated his part when she whirled on him.

"Calm down? I'm calm, Sam Callahan, but I'm about to not be!" She glared at him. "Is he all right? Does he need a doctor?"

Sabrina was frightened out of her wits. She held Joe tightly to her, and wondered what the brothers weren't telling her. Jonas still had his boots on! No man went to bed in muddy boots. She reached to feel his forehead, checking his temperature, but pulled back her hand when he opened his eyes to look at her.

"Hi," Jonas said. He glanced around at his brothers. "Why is everybody here? Did I miss the weekly meeting or something?"

Sam approached the bed. "How are you feeling, bro?"

"I feel…" he began, then squinted. Sabrina held her breath. "I feel like I've been asleep for days." He looked around the room again. "I can't believe I'm here. I thought I'd be somewhere else."

Sabrina blinked. She was almost afraid of what he might say! "Where else would you have thought you'd be?"

"I don't know." He tried to sit up, and Sam helped him until Jonas brushed him off. "You're not going to believe what happened to me."

"Happened to you?" Rafe asked.

"Yeah." Jonas swept his hair back with a hand and looked at Sabrina. "What day is it?"

She started to say *two days past our big date you big lug.* But her relief at seeing him was too great. Yet something was different about Jonas. Something had changed.

"It's Sunday, Jonas. Tell us what happened," she said.

His brothers waited, but Jonas didn't immediately reply.

"Do you think he has a concussion?" Pete asked the room at large.

"I don't have a concussion," Jonas said, appearing to

grapple with what he wanted to say. He looked around at his brothers. "You're never in a million years going to believe this, but I saw our parents."

A sharp intake of breath met his words. Sabrina saw all the brothers glance at each other, then back at Jonas.

They didn't believe him. Sabrina clutched Joe, not feeling it was her place to speak. Whatever was happening right now was between the Callahans. Her heart beat harder, like frantic hummingbird wings.

"Our parents?" Sam asked, his voice steady and low. "How could that happen, Jonas?"

"I don't know." Jonas slowly shook his head. "I just know it did. They're alive, and they're well." He lowered his voice, his eyes distant as he remembered. "It was the most surreal moment of my life, except for when I found out I was a dad."

He reached for the baby, and Sabrina handed him their son. She understood Jonas's need for his child. Holding Joe calmed her, too, when she felt unsettled.

Jonas kissed his baby on the head, closing his eyes for a moment as he breathed in his scent. "They're pretty cool people."

"Jonas," Sam said, pulling up a wooden chair to sit next to the bed. He eyed his brother sharply. "Your truck hasn't moved. Honestly, not to doubt your story, but I don't think you've left this room."

Rafe nodded. "Not that we doubt what you're saying, but what you're claiming is pretty far out."

Sabrina believed him. Jonas didn't have a concussion, he didn't have a fever, he wasn't on a bender. He'd seen something that had changed him; she could feel soul-deep peace emanating from him. "What are they like, Jonas?" she asked softly, and five Callahans swung their heads to stare at her. She could feel their astonishment that she believed their brother's improbable tale.

Jonas's gaze flashed to her just for an instant, his eyes communicating his understanding that she recognized he was completely lucid. Then he seemed to focus on baby Joe, his thoughts far away. "Mom's a lot like what I remembered. She has gray hair now, a beautiful silvery-gray. She's happy." He smiled at the memory. "And Dad is still the most energetic, amazing man I ever met. They miss us, but they're content." He glanced up to meet his brothers' stares. "They're real happy we're doing well."

The room was silent for a long time.

"Where are they?" Creed asked.

"I'm not sure where they are. I couldn't get back there if I wanted to, I don't think." He frowned.

Judah let out a sigh. "So how did you find them?"

Jonas considered his words. "I went with Running Bear."

Pete leaned his boot on the footboard. "He just randomly drove you to see people he's been hiding from us all our lives?"

"We rode Diablos," Jonas said, and the room went electric. Sabrina could feel the brothers stiffen, their attention caught.

"You rode Diablos," Sam said. "Spirit horses."

Jonas nodded. "That's exactly what happened. We rode for hours."

"Where is the Diablo you rode back, Jonas?" Rafe asked.

"I don't know," he said. He kissed little Joe on the

head again and leaned him against his chest. "When I got back from seeing Mom and Dad, Running Bear was gone. I think. I can't remember, to tell you the truth."

His words were met with silence.

"If you had no horse, how did you get home?" Creed finally asked.

Jonas's forehead wrinkled. "That's where it all gets a bit misty for me."

"Misty?" Sabrina asked. Her heart hurt for him. She knew something had happened to the man she loved, but she also knew that the story he was telling seemed so unlikely. She couldn't blame his brothers for asking a lot of questions.

"Yeah. It was so strange. I felt like I was in a dream state from the moment we got there. And when I ran down to the village, I felt like I was floating on air." Jonas's gaze turned inward. "But I knew the whole thing was more real than anything in my life when I saw Mom and Dad." He took a deep breath. "When Dad hugged me, I felt strong. I felt things I haven't felt in a long time."

His gaze met Sabrina's. She smiled at him a bit wanly. "Have you eaten since you left with Running Bear?"

He shook his head.

"Do you want anything?" she asked.

"Sleep," Jonas said, handing little Joe back to her. "I think I'll go to sleep."

"You do that, bro." Sam moved away from the bed. "Give a shout if you need anything."

Jonas barely nodded. His eyes drooped shut and his head flopped back onto the pillow, as if all the energy had flowed out of him during the telling of his adventure. They all filed from the room, Sabrina the last one to go. She didn't want to leave Jonas, but he did seem to need to rest. Quietly, she closed the door behind her and little Joe, and followed the Callahans down the stairs.

"Holy Moses," Sam said. "He's in bad shape."

The brothers drifted into the den. Not knowing what else to do, Sabrina followed them. It was Joe's father lying up there in some kind of weakened state. She felt she had a right to listen in on this conversation.

Rafe nodded. "Yeah. I've never seen him like that."

"We've always relied on Jonas to be the doctor in the family. But I think he may need one," Pete suggested.

"No," Creed said. "I say we let him rest. He's probably dehydrated and a little disoriented. When he wakes up again, we'll check him out. If he's not down here chowing like a wolf, we'll drag him to the E.R."

"I suppose it's possible he's been smoking some funny cigarettes," Judah said, shocking everyone in the room. "We all noticed he smelled like smoke. And it wasn't barroom smoke, either."

A protest rose to Sabrina's lips and died just as quickly. Jonas's brothers didn't believe him. Why did she?

Because she knew that whatever had happened to Jonas was real.

"Sabrina!"

She jumped as Jonas bellowed down the staircase.

"That didn't sound like a dehydrated man," Sam observed.

Sabrina leaped to her feet and carried little Joe

upstairs. She went into the guestroom. "You roared, Jonas?"

"Sabrina," Jonas said, taking the baby from her, "marry me. Marry me tonight."

She was astonished. "Jonas!"

Cradling their son in one arm, he tugged her onto the bed next to him. She stared at him, not certain what to think.

"You said I needed to know my past." He looked at her, his navy eyes bright with a strange light. "Well, I do. It's a part of me. It never went away all these years, though I felt like it had. But seeing my parents again—" He shook his head. "Sabrina, it was magic. I can't even explain it."

"I know," she murmured. "Your brothers don't believe it happened."

"It did. Just like I said."

She nodded. "But—"

"No buts." He took her hand and pressed it against his heart. "Sabrina, you were worried that I wouldn't make a good husband because I was too scarred, you don't have to worry anymore."

She was about to say he was right, when a huge commotion erupted downstairs. Male voices were suddenly raised, and then a female cried out.

"Stay here with Joe," Jonas said, and took off running.

Sabrina clutched her baby and went to the landing to try to see what was happening.

She heard Rafe say, "They caught him, sneaking into one of the barns."

She moved down a couple of steps so she could eavesdrop better.

"Why?" Jonas asked. "There's nothing for you here. We established that before."

"And I told you," a man's voice replied, "that eventually we would find them."

Sonny Baker. Sabrina closed her eyes, feeling the hopeful, bright beginnings of the proposal she'd received from Jonas slipping away.

"Call Sheriff Cartwright," Jonas commanded.

Knowing that the brothers probably had Sonny in a chokehold, Sabrina ventured downstairs and into the den. Chelsea stood behind the brothers, her eyes round with shock.

"Jonas, I promise I had no idea he was trying to harm your family," Chelsea said, and Sabrina felt sorry for her.

"Don't worry. You couldn't have known," Sam said quickly.

"Our parents are dead," Jonas said, his voice flat. "Anything else you've heard is a fairy tale."

Sabrina blinked. Jonas's face was set like a statue's, cold and unmoving. He looked hard and angry, and she thought Sonny should be quaking in his boots. The two foremen who'd caught Sonny shook him, making his head wobble.

Chelsea's gaze met hers, and Sabrina sent her a tiny smile to try to reassure her. Chelsea had no way of knowing what was going on; she was a stranger here who'd probably been lured by a man's attention. Likely Sonny had handed her a smooth line that would have been hard to resist. Would the nightmare ever end for the Callahans?

"Sabrina, go to Aberdeen's," Jonas said curtly.

She met his eyes, startled, and what she saw there scared her.

He looked at her as if he no longer knew her.

With his dark, icy gaze on her, Sabrina walked from the kitchen, her heart stinging from what had felt very much like a rebuke.

Chapter Eight

Jonas felt bad about the way he'd spoken to Sabrina, but he hadn't expected her to come downstairs. He didn't want Sonny to see her, didn't want him to see little Joe. Men like him, who spent years looking for people in witness protection, were capable of anything.

A nameless terror touched Jonas's heart.

It didn't abate when Sheriff Cartwright came and arrested Sonny—again—for trespassing. The charge wouldn't stick for long.

The problem had to be resolved somehow. The situation with Chelsea also required some serious thought. Thirty minutes after Cartwright dragged Baker off, Jonas leaned against a kitchen wall, aware that his five brothers were watching him like hawks.

They think I'm crazy. They think I had some kind of Wizard of Oz *dream where I woke up and thought I'd had this wonderful adventure of meeting our parents and riding a mystical Diablo.*

"Jonas," Sam said, "we've got to work some things out."

"I know." Most important among the things he planned to work out was getting Sabrina to the altar. He wondered if it was possible to lure her to Dark Diablo with Joe. Sonny wouldn't be in jail long—he'd get bail somehow, and there wasn't much Sheriff Cartwright could do about that. Jonas knew he'd return to Rancho Diablo once again.

The cold fear touched him again. He'd seen what a lifetime of hiding looked like when he'd gazed at his parents. They were calm, they were protected and happy—but he knew what they'd sacrificed.

He didn't want Sabrina and Joe in any danger, nor any of the Callahan wives and children. Sonny had said that whoever had sent him would just send someone else if they had to. Whoever was behind Sonny's mission here was determined.

Jonas looked around at his brothers, who watched him warily. "We're going to have to find out who hired Sonny."

"How are we going to do that?" Rafe asked. "He's not going to talk."

Running Bear probably knew, but Jonas had a feeling the chief had said as much as he intended to when he'd taken Jonas to see Jeremiah and Molly. "I don't know. All I know is that we need to find that out."

"Okay," Pete said. "The next question is, what are you going to do about Chelsea?"

His brothers murmured about that.

"She can't stay here, Jonas," Creed said gently.

Jonas nodded. It was true. She hadn't meant any harm, but she'd been used to get to them. Now she could be in danger, though Jonas doubted she realized it. "I'll have to tell her."

"She won't like it," Judah said. "She's happy here."

That was also true. As soon as Sabrina had left,

Chelsea had tearfully apologized for bringing someone to the ranch who had bad intent. And then she'd hurried off, murmuring that she was going to go find Sabrina.

Jonas sighed. "She might be happy here, but this isn't her home. She hasn't lived in Diablo long enough to get deeply attached. She has a mother in Ireland who'll probably be happy to have her back."

"Ireland, Ireland," Sam muttered. "Why do all trails seem to return to Ireland?"

Jonas sent his brother a sharp look, about to ask him what the hell he was talking about, when the kitchen door opened. The brothers turned, staring as two well-used suitcases came sliding through the doorway.

Jonas stiffened. If Sabrina was leaving him, he'd lose his mind.

"Ah, it feels so good to be home!" Fiona said, giving them all a bright smile as she appeared in the kitchen, Burke following close behind. "There's nothing like family, and I missed mine terribly!"

Jonas closed his eyes for a brief second as the brothers jumped to wrap their aunt and uncle in warm embraces. He listened to the happy voices, felt the joy as they crowded together in a litany of excited greetings.

But he knew, even as he went to hug Fiona, that her return was not the simple coming home of an aunt who missed her nephews. No doubt Running Bear had communicated to her what had transpired with Jonas's journey to find his parents.

"No hug from you, Jonas?" she asked, and all the brothers turned to stare at him with some surprise.

"Welcome home, Aunt Fiona," Jonas said, "Uncle

Burke. It's good to have you back." He gave them each a warm hug, then grinned down at his aunt. "I missed you when I was in Ireland."

She gave him a big smile, her eyes twinkling. "I heard you'd been there. So sorry we missed you! We did all the traveling we'd been saving up for, and now it's all out of our system. We didn't stay long in Ireland, as I'm sure you know."

He looked at her indulgently. She wasn't fooling him. "Yes, I do know."

She patted his arm. "We have a lot to talk about."

This was the woman who'd brought Sabrina into his life, hiring her to be a gypsy fortune teller who warned that Rancho Diablo was in danger. It *had* been in danger, but Fiona had used her big moment on the stage to figure out a way to get all her nephews married with children.

Her plan had been flawless.

Jonas was still unmarried, something he intended to change at the first opportunity. But Sabrina had been right; there were things he had to settle first.

And in his arms stood the main item which required settling. "Yes," he said, giving his aunt a fond kiss on her cheek, knowing now that something had happened to bring her home to drive their lives again. "Yes, we have a lot to talk about. Let me pour you a cup of tea. I'm sure you're tired after your long flight."

"It was rather long," Fiona said, looking around her kitchen as she sat in the chair Burke offered her. "Chelsea tells me you men have been keeping very busy."

Jonas turned his head. "Chelsea?"

"Mmm." Fiona sighed as she settled in. "She calls

her mother regularly. Sometimes she talked to me, too, when I was over there checking on her mum."

Jonas nodded. It all made sense now. Chelsea was another of Fiona's "hires." No wonder she'd agreed to be his fake fiancée—she'd been put on to him by Fiona. And had been keeping tabs on him and his brothers, feeding information to Fiona, who had judged the right time to return.

So now was the "right" time for something—but Jonas knew she wouldn't give up that secret any more easily than she'd given up any other.

Still, he was now the president of the Books'n'Bingo Society—and if that didn't give him the mantle of head busybody, he didn't know what would.

"So glad you're here, Aunt Fiona," Jonas said, and his brothers looked at him, watching him, probably wondering why he didn't seem like the Jonas of old who had fawned all over their little aunt.

She was stronger than she looked, Jonas knew now, probably tougher than any of them. He sat down next to her and patted her hand. Then he took a deep breath. "But I'm afraid you can't live at Rancho Diablo anymore."

A startled gasp from the brothers met his words.

"What the hell, Jonas?" Sam said.

Jonas stood. "I'm sorry. But it's the way it has to be. Aunt Fiona," he said, his voice softening, "you've worked hard for many years raising us. We appreciate everything you did, and we love you. But there's danger here now, on this very ranch, and we need to know about our parents. We need to know *everything*. There can't be any more secrets. So if you came back to protect us and hide the past, it isn't necessary. I've seen Mom and Dad. I've talked to them."

Fiona's gaze never left his.

He patted her hand again, then glanced at Burke. "I'm sorry, but the time for secrets is past."

Fiona gazed at her husband. "Burke?" she said, her voice soft and perhaps a little teary.

Burke considered Jonas for a long moment, then glanced around at the brothers, who looked as if they were set to hop all over Jonas for his treatment of their aunt. Then Burke nodded at his small, delicate wife.

"He's right, Fiona. We can let it all go now. You don't have to worry anymore."

Fiona burst into tears and hid her face in her hands. Jonas sat down next to her again, rubbing her back, and Burke knelt at her side. After a moment Jonas took his little aunt in his arms and held her tight so she'd know how much he loved her, how much they all loved her.

But Sabrina had been right—the past was part of the future. And the Callahans had a right to know what was coming.

"SO THAT'S WHAT HAPPENED," Jonas told Sabrina an hour later, after he finally found her at Aberdeen's and dragged her off to the guesthouse, where he'd been staying. They'd left little Joe with Aberdeen because he was asleep. Besides, Jonas wanted time alone with the woman who hadn't accepted his proposal.

He was well aware Sabrina hadn't thrown her arms around his neck with a delighted, "Yes, Jonas!" when he'd popped the question. Likely she was ruffled, too, because he'd barked at her. So there was work to be done.

"We decided we'll have a family meeting, after Fiona and Burke have had time to rest from their trip." Jonas shook his head. "I don't think my brothers are speaking to me right now. They thought I was a bit hard on her."

He felt Sabrina glance at him as they went inside the guesthouse. He didn't want to do anything but talk, tell her how sorry he was that he'd missed their big date night. Holding her in his arms would be good, too, but that didn't seem promising at the moment. Sabrina seemed as shell-shocked as he felt.

"I know it's getting late," she said, "but do you feel like going for a drive?"

"I do, actually." Jonas was restless. He was glad she felt like getting off the ranch. "Anywhere in particular?"

"No." She looked at him, and Jonas thought he'd never seen a more beautiful woman. Everything about Sabrina lit him up inside. But it was more than that. She seemed so much a part of him that he thought he'd go mad if she didn't agree right away to be his wife. "I'll drive if you still need to rest," she offered. "I just want to hear you talk about everything that's happened. It feels like we've been whirling in a tornado for days around here."

"No, that's okay. I'll drive." Jonas held the passenger door open so she could get in. "Do you want to go to Banger's, or do you want me to grab a cooler with water bottles and maybe some sodas?"

"Let's just start driving and see what happens," Sabrina said.

He got a couple water bottles from the fridge, attempting to avoid his brothers for the moment. Things had been uncomfortable after he'd given Aunt Fiona the ultimatum. The brothers had gone to their houses, and Fiona and Burke had gone upstairs to their old room.

Jonas just wanted to get out of Dodge.

"Okay, we're set." He got in, started his truck and drove to the end of the driveway. "Which way?"

"Let's head into town first," Sabrina suggested. "It's where we would have gone if we'd been able to get together the other night."

He sent her a glance. "You know I wouldn't have missed our date if—"

"I know." She nodded. "I knew when you didn't show up that something important had happened."

He stopped when they had barely pulled out of the long driveway. "I have the strangest feeling that only you believe me about seeing our folks. My brothers hardly asked me about them, as if they don't believe me."

"I think they were in shock. From an outsider's perspective, I don't think they knew what to say. By now they've probably got a million questions they want to ask. But then Sonny showed up, and that was awful, and Fiona and Burke came home. There was just so much at one time they're trying to process. It was all pretty crazy. Your trip to your folks sounded like a dream," she said, her voice apologetic, "and I don't think they knew what to think."

Jonas snapped his fingers. "That reminds me! I forgot my cell phone."

"I've got mine," Sabrina said, holding up her purse. "Aberdeen will call me if Joe needs anything."

He looked at Sabrina. "Not that I want to prolong us getting out on our date, but would you mind if I make a detour?"

Sabrina smiled at him, and he felt warmed inside.

"I don't care where we go," she said.

"Good." Jonas turned right, and drove over Rancho Diablo land through the darkness. "Horseback would be better, but we'll do date night on horseback another time."

She laughed, not sounding worried at all. "At least date night with you isn't dull."

"I can be romantic, too," Jonas said. "Just wait. One day it's going to be just me and you, and a bearskin rug or something. That thought is what keeps me going."

"Me, too," Sabrina said, and Jonas felt hopeful that she meant maybe one day they could get back to the way they'd been before. Although no more friendly sex, he told himself. She was going to have to make love to him wearing a gold ring on her hand, whether she liked it or not.

"Here we are."

"Wow," Sabrina said, getting out of the truck. "The middle of nowhere."

"Never let it be said I didn't take you anyplace nice," Jonas answered, grabbing a flashlight from the glove compartment.

"I won't." Sabrina came around the vehicle. "Are we looking for a body?"

"Just my cell phone," Jonas said, heading to the cave.

"Your cell phone is out here in the armpit of the ranch?"

He grinned to himself. "Be careful where you step."

"Believe me, I am. I smell horse pretty thickly. Where are we?"

"Near the canyons." Jonas found the cave opening and turned to take Sabrina's hand. "How do you feel about bats?"

"Not too happy," she admitted, but she didn't pull her hand away. "I heard they prefer men to women, so they can have you for snack, and I'll head back to the ranch."

"That's my sweet girl," Jonas said, entering the cave. "Lucky for you, there haven't been any bats in here that I've ever seen." He shone the flashlight around. "Everything's just the way it was a few days ago."

Sabrina followed him over to the large, flat rock. He knelt down to dig around under it, and pulled out his phone with a grin. "Exactly where I left it. I like it when that happens, don't you?"

Sabrina blinked. "You left your phone in a cave? Why? So you couldn't be tracked?"

"I guess so." Jonas shrugged. "At the time, I didn't think too much about it. I just did what the chief told me."

Sabrina sat on the rock, watching him as he took his phone out of the plastic bag and switched it on. "So the chief was your guide on your journey?"

"Mmm." Jonas stared at his phone. "Cell service is very spotty and almost nonexistent in this cave. But I see you left me about six texts."

She gave him an arch look. "I was annoyed."

"Were you now?" He slid up beside her on the rock and stuffed his phone in his jeans' pocket. "You do strike me as being a very impatient woman."

"I just thought you were a lousy date."

"But a great father." He kissed her on the mouth, searching her lips for the affection he knew she felt for him. Even though she was trying to hide her feelings at the moment, Jonas knew Sabrina was crazy about him. "And I'll be a great husband when you finally drag me to the altar."

"I drag *you?*" She pulled away from him. "I don't think so, cowboy."

He tugged her into his lap and nuzzled her neck. "It's a deal I wouldn't pass up if I were you, lady."

"You're not me."

"Thankfully. I like being the guy who gets to make love to you."

"Lots of talk, very little action these days." But it seemed her heart wasn't in the banter. She slipped off his lap and Jonas reluctantly let her go. "I feel like we shouldn't stay here," Sabrina said, rubbing her arms. "Something's making me feel a little strange."

"I hope it's me," Jonas said, getting up to follow her from the cave. "I hope what you're feeling is how-fast-can-I-tear-off-his-clothes hot for me."

"I don't think so." She glanced around outside the cave, her gaze searching.

She sounded so distant. "If you're worried about little Joe, we can go back."

"Let's go, Jonas," Sabrina said urgently, and it hit him that she was scared. He didn't know if she was having a flash of clairvoyance or if she was just spooked. He said, "Hop to it, gorgeous," and they ran to the truck, jumping in. Sabrina locked the doors immediately.

"What was that all about?" Jonas asked.

"I don't know," Sabrina said. "I had the funniest sensation we weren't alone. Drive, Jonas, please."

He turned on the truck and peeled away from the cave, his breath tight in his chest, his heart thundering like mad. "Sabrina, are you afraid of me?"

"Don't be a dope," she said, staring around them in the darkness. "We weren't alone, Jonas."

"Let me go back and see who it was, then," he said.

"No!" Sabrina leaned her head back against the seat. "Let's just go to Banger's."

"Feeling like a brewski?" He did. Sabrina had him worried. She sounded jangled and frightened.

"Absolutely," she said. "Maybe two."

He reached for her wrist, pulling her hand into his lap to comfort her. "Maybe I'll get you tipsy and have my way with you."

"Maybe you will," Sabrina said, "but probably not."

He laughed. "Always my sweet girl."

BANGER'S WAS HOPPING, and Sabrina was thrilled to be around other people. Normal people who weren't deeply mired in a mystery, as she was starting to feel.

Out of control was the best way to describe it. With a heavy dose of fear thrown in.

"Great," she said to Jonas, "look at the hot wall art Banger's put up."

Everywhere the eye traveled were big posters of the

Callahans in all their handsome glory, and her Callahan with his sexy butt on display for every woman in town to drool over.

Jonas grinned as he slid into a booth next to her. "Looks good to me."

She gave him a wry look. "And I'm sure it looks good to every female for miles around."

"You have to admit little Joe is quite the model," Jonas teased. "Look at those cheeks hanging over my very broad shoulder."

"I'll admit Joe is darling."

"And Joe's father?"

"I'd describe him as aggravating."

Lacey walked by and tossed him a smile. "I never get tired of looking at that poster, Jonas. Some of the guys have suggested using your butt for a darts target, but every woman in this place told them they'd get no beer for a week if they so much as laid a hand on those sexy cheeks."

"You mean Joe's cheeks, I'm sure, Lacey," Sabrina said, and Jonas laughed.

"Sure, whatever." Lacey gave Jonas a wink and sashayed off.

Sabrina sipped from the glass of cold beer that had been placed in front of her. "So now what happens?"

He raised his glass to her before drinking. "Now I do my best to get you in bed at the first opportunity, beautiful."

She shook her head, not about to give him the benefit of a smile. "I mean with your family. Your guide didn't take you on your journey just to have you stop now."

Jonas looked at her. "What are you saying?"

"Haven't you been on a spiritual journey?"

He rubbed his beard. "Just with you. The next journey I intend to take is our honeymoon."

"Focus, Jonas." Sabrina tapped his hand, and he caught her fingers in his, kissing them.

"I'm pretty sure I'm focused as hard as I can be on the only thing that matters in my life."

That was so sweet it nearly distracted Sabrina from her train of thought. But then she caught herself, telling herself not to be sidetracked by the handsome man, his sex appeal and the vision of his jeans-clad butt on the wall behind him.

"Your journey isn't over," she said softly. "You can't stop here."

"I'm feeling pretty good about things. What I feel best about is that you believe me. Trust me, I could tell my brothers didn't believe a word I said, but you did."

"I don't know that they didn't believe you," Sabrina said, knowing full well his brothers hadn't.

"They didn't," Jonas said cheerfully, grabbing a chip from the straw basket that was placed on the table by a bouncy waitress named Sue. She grinned widely at Jonas, and Sabrina shot her a frown.

"Sorry, hon," Sue said, "don't get your skirt in a bunch. My Ned would kill me if I looked at another man. But that poster is just so like-father-like-son it makes me grin. And since the same picture's been put up on a billboard along the highway outside of town, we've been getting all kind of newcomers coming in, wanting to know about the Diablo Heartbreakers."

"Aw," Jonas said. "It's just we've both got great booties, me and my boy. And Sabrina's isn't bad, either," he added, accepting the compliment with more levity than he normally possessed. Sabrina stared at him, wondering where this newly loquacious Jonas had come from.

"You know," Jonas said, not holding back on the humility, "I fully expect little Joe to be holy hell in the saddle."

"Whew," Sue said. "I'll have to keep my boots shined up for the next fifteen or so years until he can rodeo. What'll you have, hot stuff?"

"Nachos," Jonas said. "Beef, everything on."

"And you, Sabrina?" Sue asked.

Sabrina wasn't sure she could eat with all the sucking up to Jonas's ego going on. "I'll try your Diablo salad, please."

"Watching those carbs, are you? Smart choice. I would, too, if I was trying to make Jonas my mister." Sue nodded. "Will you have low-fat dressing on the side?"

"Yes," Sabrina said with a sigh.

Jonas patted her hand. "Don't worry. I like my woman with a little extra padding."

"I don't know how you're gonna tie him down, honey," Sue said, going off with their orders.

Sabrina arched a brow at Jonas. "We'll skip the padding comment and go back to the spiritual journey. I believe it affects little Joe's future, maybe even more than yours."

Jonas shook his head. "Tonight I'd rather talk about your body. Actually, I want to know what you're going to do about my marriage proposal." He lifted her hand to his lips. "I think Sue may be right. You should tie me down at the first opportunity."

"What would you do, Jonas, if I actually said yes?"

He raised a brow. "Drag you off to bed?"

That sounded pretty good to her, too, actually. "I just think you're on a roll here. Taking time to get married would stop your journey."

"I'm done with journeys. I'm not traveling anyplace other than Dark Diablo."

Sabrina shook her head. "That's part of the journey, too."

"Okay," Jonas said, "if I give you five more minutes to chat about guides and journeys, would you then give me a serious shot at undressing you?"

She wrinkled her nose. If he only knew how much restraint she was exercising, he wouldn't ask the question. "Perhaps."

He smiled happily as his food was placed in front of him. "You shouldn't have ordered rabbit food," he said, casting an eye at her salad. "You'll need your strength to keep up with me."

"So Fiona was your first guide," Sabrina began, and Jonas shook his head.

"You can stop right there. I can refute that right off the top. Fiona is no guide. She is a trickster in the journey of life."

Sabrina laughed. "Your aunt would be hurt if she heard you say that!"

He bit into a nacho and closed his eyes for a moment. "These never get old. I could eat them every day. Anyway, Fiona never told us the truth about anything. She obfuscated, if you prefer that word to trickster. You can't argue the point, since she hired you as one of her first obfuscations that involved trying to get us all to the altar."

That was true, Sabrina thought with a wince. "Still, a guide teaches and shows the way. She showed you the way, though she didn't show you a straight path."

"Your five minutes is nearly up," Jonas said, sipping beer with deep contentment. "I wouldn't waste it all on Fiona, if I were you."

"All right. Your next guide was Running Bear."

Jonas waved. "Go on. Explain."

"He took you wherever you were. Whatever you really saw, he knew you were ready to see. Even though you're avoiding it now." She stabbed some of her salad and munched on it, realizing she was hungry. "This *is* delicious. And you know, your backside really isn't half-bad in that poster. I'm surprised there isn't a major traffic stoppage on the highway into town."

Jonas put his nacho down and looked at her. "What do you mean, avoiding it now?"

She waved her fork. "With all this talk about marriage, and my body, and anything but what happened. It's like you don't want to think about it. If it was me, I'd be pretty freaked out. I mean, seeing your parents after not seeing them for thirty-some-odd years had to have been mind-bending. And don't you think it's a little crazy that Sonny came back tonight? Not to mention Fiona. It feels weirdly like a tornado converging around Fate."

Jonas didn't move. He just sat there staring at her, his eyes wide, his face frozen. "I'm aware that you think I have an avoidance complex—"

"Not really—"

"And I do, it's one of my best traits. It's served me well all my life. I think sex would clear my head." But he said it so halfheartedly that Sabrina just waited. "Maybe it was a tornado, Sabrina. A *Wizard of Oz* thing, like my brothers said."

"If that's what you want to believe." Sabrina didn't, and she knew Jonas didn't, either, not really. She shrugged and went back to her salad. "I think what happened is exactly what you told us in the first place."

Chapter Nine

The door to Banger's opened and Chelsea hurried in, looking panicked.

"Sit down, Chelsea," Sabrina said, and she did automatically.

"Jonas," she said in a rush, "I am so sorry. I wouldn't have done a thing to hurt you or your brothers. I had no idea who Sonny was. He'd been hanging around, and he asked me out on a date." She took a deep breath. "I figured everyone in town knew you, and you probably knew him, so it never occurred to me that taking him to Rancho Diablo was... I had no idea he was an enemy. I'm so sorry."

"It wasn't your fault, Chelsea," Jonas said, and Sabrina was glad to hear the kindness in his voice. "Sonny's a snake in the grass. He preys on people to get what he wants. You couldn't have known."

Chelsea looked stricken. "I just want you to know that I've decided to go back home. I feel like I've abused your hospitality. And I miss Mum. I'll be better off in my own country, I think."

"You're doing fine here, Chelsea," Sabrina said. "You've made a lot of friends in Diablo."

"And one bad friend." Chelsea sounded as if she wanted to cry.

Sabrina shook her head. "Don't go just because of Sonny, Chelsea. He could have picked anyone in this town to take advantage of. He just chose you because you're sweet and kind. All of us can see that."

"Still, it would be best if I went back."

"Chelsea," Jonas said, "I'm aware that my aunt hired you to spy on us."

Chelsea smiled. "She didn't really put it that way."

"Fiona doesn't have to. Everyone knows what she wants," he said gruffly.

"She said 'keep an eye on my boys and give me an update occasionally.' That was it, Jonas, I promise." Chelsea shook her head. "You and your brothers are all so suspicious of your aunt! But she's so darling!"

"I know," Jonas said. "It's how she gets all of us to jump through hoops for her. No, Chelsea, if anybody took advantage of anyone, we took advantage of you. And as my ex-fiancée, you're entitled to some consideration for your trouble."

"I agree," Sabrina said. "What did you have in mind, Jonas?"

"I was thinking airplane tickets," Jonas said, "so you can see the country the way you said you wanted to."

"For her and her mother," Sabrina said. "If she's well enough to travel, that is, don't you think, Jonas?"

"Absolutely. A fine idea."

Chelsea stared at them, her eyes huge. "Do you mean it?"

"I do," Jonas said. "You've been a good friend to this family, and you got caught in all our dirty laundry. The least we can do is show you some beautiful places in America."

"Diablo is beautiful," Chelsea said.

"Of course," Sabrina said, "but you shouldn't leave without seeing something besides Diablo. There's New York, and California, and Virginia, and Florida...."

"I'll do it," Chelsea said, thrilled. "My mom will love this! Thank you! I can't wait to call and tell her. Thank you, Jonas!"

Chelsea shot out of the booth and hurried off. Sabrina turned to look at her cowboy. "That was sweet of you, Jonas."

"It was the least we could, considering what we put her through, thanks to your so-called guide, Fiona."

Sabrina smiled and went back to her salad. "You know you love Fiona."

"I do, but she's going to drive us all crazy." He sighed and pushed his nachos away. "I'll tell you a secret."

"I'm listening."

"I don't know where I was, or how to get back there."

Suddenly, Sabrina wasn't hungry anymore, either. "Does it matter?"

"I want to prove to my brothers that our parents are alive."

"I don't think you can," Sabrina said. "They'll figure it out when the time comes."

"This is true." Jonas nodded. "The whole thing seems like a dream, as you said. I think Running Bear was blowing some funny smoke my way that made me hallucinate. I'm even questioning myself now."

"Maybe you shouldn't doubt what you know in your

heart," Sabrina said softly. "Do you want to know what I think?"

"I want to know if you're going to marry me," Jonas said, "because I'm pretty sure you're trying to kill me. But other than that, what do you think?"

"I think you made Chelsea happy. You gave her a wonderful gift, and it's so kind of you to include her mother. You've changed a lot from the first time I met you. You were all suspicious and talking like a bad boy—"

"I fainted when you jingled your charms at me. How bad boy is that?"

"I think you had a virus or something, Jonas. You certainly didn't faint because of me." She smiled at him benignly. "Anyway, you weren't who you are now. You were all out of order in your life."

"Whatever," he said. "I was a calm, successful surgeon then. I came home for Christmas, and you laid me out with your sexual allure. It was like being whomped by a big bear. Only you were this little bitty redhead with nice, big—"

"So now," Sabrina said, interrupting, "you've made Chelsea happy, and you've put Sonny back in jail—"

"For probably eight hours," Jonas groused. "He's got staying power. I may bury him in the canyons."

"And Bode's happy, now that Julie and Rafe have given him grandkids, so that's enemy number one in your corner now," Sabrina said.

"Yeah." Jonas scratched his head. "The twins softened up that old coot considerably."

"And you've found your parents. So you see?" Sabrina ran a gentle hand down his arm. "Everything has nearly come full circle. You're even a dad now, and little Joe is going to grow up following you around all over the place. All these changes have made you a different person from the grumpy, suspicious, *unhappy* man I met so long ago."

"I was unhappy," Jonas said, "because I could tell you were up to no good, little gypsy." He leaned over and kissed her cheek. "Amazing how much alike you and Fiona are."

"I take that as a compliment. Anyway, all that's left for you to do, as I see it, is for you to forgive your aunt," Sabrina said. "Jonas, you just can't kick her off the ranch."

He paid the tab and stood. "My gypsy love, harsh as it may sound to you, the man you think has changed so much hasn't really changed it all. I'm still a grumpy, suspicious fellow at times. And if my little aunt doesn't come across with the information we need to settle our lives, it's off the ranch she goes."

Sabrina didn't say anything. But she could hardly blame Jonas. He was on a path to right the Callahan course, and he was going to do what he had to do.

She just hoped he still wanted to marry her when he knew the truth.

CORINNE ABERNATHY BEAMED at Fiona, delighted that her friend had returned from Ireland. The four women sat in the Books'n'Bingo Society's tearoom catching up, one day after Fiona's surprise return. "Fiona, the poster campaign is a smashing success. And you've come home! I have new babies in my life. Life could not be sweeter!"

Fiona sighed. "I don't know. Jonas says I can't stay if I don't do certain things I don't know if I want to do."

"Pooh!" Mavis Night said. "He doesn't mean that, Fiona. You know he doesn't."

"He does," she replied. "Jonas has changed. He used to be Mr. Nice Worrywart. Now he's Mr. My-Way-or-the-Highway-wart." She thought about it for a moment. "He has lots of warts, in my opinion." She sniffed, a little hurt that her nephew would lay down the law to her so sternly. "Mind you, he needed some backbone. I just didn't want to be the recipient of his new outlook."

"Still," Nadine Waters said, "Jonas loves you."

"I know," Fiona stated, "but he's a man on a mission."

"Can't you tell him you've got jet lag and that he needs to relax for a week?" Corinne asked. "It would give you enough time to plot whatever you think you need to do."

"You know we'll help you any way we can," Nadine said. "We haven't had a good plot around here in days."

"Not since we talked your nephews into giving us some fanny shots for business," Mavis said. "That was a stroke of genius, if I do say so myself."

"True." Corinne nodded. "Fiona, even you wouldn't have thought of that one!"

"No," Fiona said, "and whose bright idea was it to elect Jonas the president of our club?" Secretly, she was proud of him for accepting the post. "You do realize that's just one more place he and I are going to be at loggerheads?"

Corinne smiled. "It was the only way we could think of to keep him here in Diablo."

Fiona straightened. "Keep him here! What are you talking about?"

Her three friends stared at her.

"Didn't you know?" Corinne asked, her gaze curious behind her polka-dotted spectacles. "Jonas bought Dark Diablo. He's planning to move out there. My guess is he moves as soon as he figures out how to drag Sabrina and little Joe with him."

"Sabrina and little Joe?" Fiona fanned herself. "They belong in Diablo. This is home."

"That's what we tried to tell him," Nadine said, placing cookies on the scalloped plate in front of them. They sat untouched—no one was in the mood for treats. "We told Jonas we need a heart surgeon right here in Diablo."

"Indeed." Fiona pursed her lips. "Why hasn't he married Sabrina, anyway? I was going to ask, but I was afraid he'd bite my head off."

Corinne shrugged. "He's asked about ten times. Sabrina tells him no. She says she wants to marry for love, not just because of little Joe. And Jonas hasn't exactly been Mr. Romance, according to her."

"Oh, fiddle, your niece is just making things more complicated," Fiona said crustily. "Any right-minded girl would jump at the chance to marry Jonas." She wrinkled her nose. "I guess it's an aunt's prerogative to support her nephews, even when they're trying to kick her out of the house."

"If Sabrina and Jonas move to Dark Diablo, that's just the way it goes," Mavis said. "When I got married, I moved three states away from my parents."

"Yes, but a good heart surgeon is worth his weight

in gold," Nadine pointed out. "There's lots of old hearts in this town."

"But Jonas is stubborn, like his aunt." Mavis finally took a cookie covered in pink sprinkles. "I don't know what's keeping Sabrina from getting into her own magic wedding dress."

Fiona's brows shot up. "That's right! That *is* Sabrina's gown! It was her mother's, something she was given in some foreign country by someone who said it was magic. Of course, no one in this town believes in fairy tales…." Her voice trailed off as she glanced around at her friends.

"Just mystical Diablos and magic wedding gowns and Native American spirit lore," Nadine countered. "Heavens, just about any good bit of Irish fairy dust gets us going, doesn't it?"

Fiona beetled her brows at her friend, wondering if she detected sarcasm. They each took a sip of tea while she regrouped. "I don't know about you ladies, but perhaps what this town needs is a magic wedding gown rescue."

Corinne blinked. "Rescue?"

Fiona nodded. "Maybe Sabrina needs to be rescued by her own gown, the one she so kindly shared with all the ladies who are now just waiting to be her new sisters-in-law. It would be the right thing to do for little Joe," she finished triumphantly.

The other women nodded.

"I'm game," Corinne said.

"I'm in," Mavis said. "Whatever it takes to keep them here."

"I could never resist a well-done plot," Nadine said. "Helping people is in my blood!"

Fiona sat back, smiling at her friends who had never let her down.

"So, Jonas," Fiona said.

It was midnight, but Fiona didn't look tired. She looked as if she had multiple things on her mind. Jonas relaxed in the upstairs library, thinking that if he played his cards right and all went well between him and his aunt, he might just slide down the hall and get into bed with Sabrina.

Little Joe slept in a crib in the room. He was a sound sleeper, having figured out early on how to slumber all through the night. Surely he wouldn't mind if his father made slow, gentle love to his mother.

The thought made Jonas's temples pound.

"Yes, Aunt Fiona?" he said. "You wanted to speak with me?"

She gave him a knowing look. "I think you want to speak with me. I seem to recall something about me being sent back to Ireland if I don't have a chat with you. So let's chat."

He nodded, relieved the moment had finally arrived. "Aunt, I love you. We all do. And we're very grateful for all you've done. But we need to know everything you've been trying to protect us from over the years."

She leaned back, her doughy face unsmiling. He thought she looked small and spare in her blue-flowered dress and her brown walking shoes.

"Well," Fiona said, "you think you saw your parents. We can start there."

"I did see our parents." He nodded. "Go on. I'm listening."

Fiona took a deep breath. "This is hard for me to talk about. It's been a secret for so long that I'm scared to speak it aloud."

Jonas glanced around. He started to say that no one could hear them, that the house was secure. But he didn't really know that, not with the way Sonny had managed to sneak around. Besides Chelsea, Sabrina, little Joe and Burke, they were the only people in the house currently. "I think it's safe enough."

"All right." Fiona thought for a moment, studying Jonas. Then she said, "Your parents didn't want to leave you boys."

"I know."

"They informed on a cartel that was engaged in drug trafficking. Your father was trying to protect the tribe—his tribe—and also Rancho Diablo, which was becoming something of a thoroughfare for the cartel. It was very dangerous here." Fiona's gaze remained steady on his. "Raising a family here alone, so far from anything, was difficult. You have to understand that Diablo was barely a speck on the map at the time."

"It's barely a speck now."

She nodded. "So it was basically your folks here and the Jenkinses on the place next door. Very lonely, very desolate. Your parents had little choice but to try to save their home and land. Your father was determined that no one was going to take from the tribe and from you boys what was rightfully yours. And your father also felt a responsibility to Diablo. If he hadn't acted, Diablo would not be the town it is today. I doubt it would even be here. There certainly wouldn't be tourists and the like." She gave Jonas a long look. "Imagine no churches, no safe schools for children to learn in. No hospital, no Banger's. That may be hard for you to envision, but that's the future your father saw. Nothing but devastation and danger for miles around." She shrugged. "It was one man, one woman, against a determined cartel. There was really no choice. And for what it's worth, my sister backed your dad one hundred percent in informing." Fiona's eyes glittered for just a moment, as if misty tears might be gathering, but she wasn't about to cry. "Molly and Jeremiah knew that once they informed and helped set up a sting, there would be no turning back. And there wasn't."

Jonas's blood grew chilled. The amount of sacrifices his parents had endured had been great—almost too great. He swallowed. "What happened?"

"They worked with the government. It wasn't too much of a stretch, since your father had been in the military, anyway."

"He was?"

Fiona nodded. "He'd been a code breaker. Very simple to understand that would be his chosen profession. Jeremiah's a smart man. And I don't mind saying that I understood my sister's love for your brother. When you're the daughters of parents who went through the Trouble in Ireland, you appreciate something of a good fight. A cause is easily embraced if it's right—and it's in your blood."

Jonas felt as if he was hearing the life story of someone else. His life had been so peaceful that it was hard to imagine what had been swirling around him as a child. "And then?"

Fiona slowly shook her head. "They went straight into witness protection. There was no other way, although they hadn't realized that before. Still, they wouldn't have changed what they did." She hesitated for a long moment, then said, "They couldn't take you boys with them, of course. Five children is a fairly unusual number and would have been a giveaway wherever they went. And I'm sure you've figured out that Molly was pregnant when they went into the program. But they didn't want Sam separated from you boys, so they sent him here after he was born."

Jonas ached for his parents. "Sam always wondered if he was one of us, if he was a true Callahan."

She nodded. "He is. Giving him up was as excruciating as giving up all of you. Still," Fiona said, "I'm proud of what they did."

It was pretty stunning. Jonas thought about his parents, the memories he had of his childhood, and came up with smiles, big warm hugs, happy laughter. "I had no idea. Life just seemed to be about squabbling with my brothers and getting excited about the newest horses Dad brought home."

"There was no reason for you kids to know. It was impossible, anyway. You couldn't have helped, and would have only been scared. Believe me, your father was scared enough for ten men." Fiona thought for a moment, then said, "Scared is the wrong word, because Jeremiah's probably the bravest man I know. Burke's pretty brave, too, but Jeremiah was willing to spit in the eye of the devil if he had to. Your father was angry, wild with anger, over what was happening here. He didn't want to see the land destroyed. And he wasn't about to let some dirty cowards ruin his life."

"Didn't they?" Jonas asked.

"Aren't you a heart surgeon?" Fiona shot back. "You kids had everything you ever needed. Your lives were better because of what your father did. How were your parents' lives ruined?"

"Because they couldn't be here with us."

"They were," Fiona stated. "They were always here with you. Perhaps they weren't able to take you to the ice cream parlor every weekend. Maybe they weren't able to watch your plays at school. But your folks didn't desert you boys. They always knew everything you were doing."

"Running Bear," Jonas said.

Fiona nodded. "Yes. He set up a way to get information back and forth to your parents. I'll put Running Bear up there on the Bravest Men list."

"Baby pictures," Jonas said. "He put photos of the new Callahan children in the cave."

"Right. There was a runner, a night rider, who came at specified times and transferred money, communications, whatever. I know you've discovered the silver box in the basement, Jonas."

He shrugged. "After a while, we began to suspect that it didn't hold the dead body that our active imaginations had dreamed up. We entertained ourselves with some pretty spooky stories over the years."

She shook her head, looking not at all surprised. "One of you boys should have turned out to be a writer. Anyway, we knew Sonny was living in the canyons—

we didn't know his name, of course. We just knew there was a mercenary down there. Burke and Running Bear found him, kept tabs on him. We let him live," Fiona said. "It was easier to deal with the devil we knew than for them to send another one. We knew his ways, knew how to outsmart him."

"Holy smokes," Jonas said. "You've been in danger this whole time, Aunt Fiona."

"I wouldn't say danger," she said. "Remember, I had Burke looking out for me. And besides, who was going to suspect a frail, little old woman of pitting her wits against a hired mercenary?"

Jonas laughed out loud. "Sonny had no idea what he was up against."

"I wasn't worried about him. I was worried about my sister, and her husband, and you kids. The thought of danger to me never entered my mind," she said, her tone starchy.

"Fiona, we owe you a lot. I take back every word I said about kicking you out," Jonas said, meaning it.

"I was wondering when you were going to want to know badly enough to insist. Frankly, Jonas, I thought you'd have dragged it out of me sooner. You boys have all been so slow about asking questions."

"Slow!" Jonas stared at his aunt. "You and Burke were closed up tighter than Fort Knox whenever we did ask a question!"

She smiled, obviously pleased. "We did our part, I hope."

"So what does Sonny want now? To kill our parents?"

"Yes," Fiona said. "That's what he was hired to do."

Jonas's blood went to instant boil. "I'll kill him."

"You won't," Fiona said, "because little Joe needs his father. Let the land take its own vengeance."

"What does that mean?"

"It means," she said slowly, "that Running Bear is your grandfather. He is your father's father. The tribe isn't going to let anything happen to your folks."

"Grandfather?" Jonas asked in surprise. Then again, he supposed he really shouldn't be so amazed by the revelation. Now that he thought about it, Jeremiah did resemble Running Bear in a lot of ways. "We thought he was just a drinking buddy of yours, Aunt."

"Drinking buddy?" She tried not to smile at his teasing. "You boys were always a little on the imaginative side."

"He showed up every Christmas Eve, like clockwork. We figured it was for the eggnog."

Fiona gave Jonas a wry look. "Like I would give Running Bear eggnog for Christmas. Nothing less than Corinne's homemade wine! Or whiskey, if Corinne's vines didn't produce that year."

"So he's my grandfather. Our grandfather." Jonas smiled, proud of his family relation. "I've always liked the chief."

"I'm surprised you didn't figure it out sooner. You're his spitting image. With shorter hair, of course." She looked at Jonas, considering his grown-out mane. "You're looking less surgeon these days and more renegade."

"It's the little woman," Jonas said. "I don't have time for the barber. I can't get Sabrina to the altar, so I spend all my time trying to convince her. Believe me, it's a full-time job."

Fiona nodded. "Slow as usual. It's all right, Jonas. Everything happens in its right time."

He smiled. "Can't rush a good thing. As far as I'm concerned, Sabrina's a very good thing." Glancing toward the library windows, he saw that the moon was high in a sky studded with stars. "I should let you get to bed."

"Oh, so you don't need the whole story in one sitting?" Fiona said. "You'll let me drag it out for a few days, in respect for my advanced age?"

Jonas laughed. "Or mine."

Fiona pressed her lips together. "Don't coddle me, Jonas Callahan."

"I'm not. I wouldn't dream of it. But morning chores are at five, or four, depending on how fast I can get out of bed." Jonas stood. "Anyway, you've given me a lot to think about."

"As thinkers go, you're not exactly lightning." Fiona accepted his kiss on her cheek. "And you're not fooling me, Jonas. I'm going down that hall and I'll close my door. Then you may leave the library."

"Deal." He grinned at her. "Scurry."

"I'll do no such thing, no matter how anxious you are." She shot him a look as she went. "I might remind you that sleeping babies do not like to be awakened. Burke and I made certain you boys stayed in your beds until it was time for chores."

"That's what you thought, Aunt Fiona. As soon as your eyelids slammed shut, we were usually down the tree branch, down a rope or down the drainpipe."

She stared at him. "We wondered why you never tried to sneak down the stairs."

He gave her a hug. "We knew you needed your rest after chasing us around all day."

She moved along the hall. "You realize Running Bear was usually on sentry, keeping an eye on you rascals."

Jonas hesitated. "Are you pulling my leg?"

"Do I look like I pull legs on a regular basis?"

"A sentry?" Jonas stared at his aunt, trying to decide if she was having fun at his expense.

Fiona smiled. "Six boys are eventually destined to try to sow some wild oats. We were determined that the oats sown would not be any wilder than appropriate. Running Bear was always with you, no matter where you boys ventured off to."

Jonas thought about that. "My brothers and I always thought it was a ghost. We thought there were ghosts at Rancho Diablo."

"I know." Fiona's laughter floated back to him as she went into her bedroom. "Rancho Diablo has its fair share of ghosts, but it always had its fair share of boys with very vivid imaginations, too."

Jonas shook his head as he waited until he heard her door close and lock. Not letting another second slip away from him, he went to Sabrina's door, quietly opening it.

The room smelled like baby powder. Jonas smiled. There was a tiny night-light near little Joe, and the moon shone through the window, as well, illuminating Sabrina. The smile left Jonas's face, his joy being replaced by a hungrier emotion.

He took off his boots and clothes and slid into bed, fitting himself up against her and snaking an arm around her waist.

"Jonas?" she said sleepily as he buried his face against her neck.

"Mmm." She did not smell like baby powder. She smelled like warm, beautiful woman. He'd been with her like this many times—and he missed it like fire.

"Oh, Jonas," Sabrina said, her voice soft as she turned to him. "It's about time you got into my bed."

Chapter Ten

"Go back to sleep, beautiful," Jonas said. "I didn't mean to wake you."

Go back to sleep? How did he propose she do that? With his strong arms holding her and his warm body crushed up against hers, the last thing on her mind was rest.

"If you didn't mean to wake me up, what are you doing in my bed?" Sabrina asked, wishing his mind was on the same thing as hers.

"Hiding from my family." He nestled his face in her hair and inhaled deeply. "And keeping an eye on little Joe."

He was crazy if he thought he could wind her up and then refuse to do anything about it. At least he could spare some kisses! "Look, Jonas—"

"Shh," he whispered. "You're going to wake the baby."

Wake the baby! Little Joe could sleep through a college football game. She was up, and she wanted Jonas to quit being so reluctant. "Jonas—"

Gentle snoring in her ear brought the abrupt realization that romance from her Romeo was out of the question. She thought about shaking him, then decided he'd sounded distinctly not in the mood for lovemaking.

In fact, he'd sounded weary.

Weary wasn't good. Maybe after Jonas had rested, he'd wake up a bit more like his old, passionate self. And being held was nice. Closing her eyes, Sabrina allowed herself to relax in his embrace, welcoming the feel of his hard body. She'd missed this.

But when Jonas did open those big blue eyes of his, she certainly hoped he would remember that, once upon a time, he'd never gotten in her bed without a certain sexy mission in mind.

ABOUT 3:00 A.M. A WAIL from little Joe made Sabrina's eyes fly open. She started to untangle herself from Jonas.

"I got it," he said. "Go back to sleep."

The warmth and comfort left her as Jonas got out of bed. Sabrina turned over to watch him handle his son for the first time in the middle of the night. Given the night-light and the slight crack between the wooden blinds, she had a fairly good view of Jonas's long, lean body in black boxer shorts that were fitted to his muscled legs. His back curved protectively as he gathered his distressed son in his arms.

Probably surprised at being picked up by someone other than Sabrina, Joe ceased crying immediately.

"Little Joe," Jonas murmured, "that was some commotion you raised. I can tell you have your uncle Sam's lungs. And your uncle Rafe's penchant for drama. Possibly even your uncle Creed's love of creating a disturbance just for the sake of drawing attention to himself.

But don't you worry, little man, everything in your world is just fine."

Jonas kissed his baby on the head, then did a fast diaper change, which astounded Sabrina. He picked Joe up again, cradling him against his chest, and then rocked him from side to side, rubbing his back. Joe calmed almost instantly, and tears jumped into Sabrina's eyes, she was so touched by Jonas's care with his son.

"Now, Joe," Jonas said, his voice husky and soft, "I'm going to tell you a family secret right off the bat, so you won't inherit any weirdness from your uncles. Uncle Pete is afraid of ghosts, but the ones around here are friendly and mostly of the mental variety, anyway. The ladies say Uncle Judah is the most handsome of all of us, but you've got him beat by a mile in looks and personality. So don't be afraid of your uncles. They all love you and want to help you. You're a pretty secure fellow, so there's no reason to get your diaper in a twist over night phantoms. Trust me, if your gnarly uncles can survive their human foibles, you're in great shape to grow up to be one well-balanced dude." He kissed his son's head once again. "Now, you let your mother sleep, and if you're a good boy, tomorrow I'll take you to the library for a book. It's about time we get started on *The Odyssey*. Perhaps Benjamin Franklin's book on frugality. We're a bit behind on your education, but we can get you caught up in no time." He gently laid the baby in the crib and covered him with a soft blanket.

After a moment, when Joe didn't move again, Jonas left the room. Sabrina's astonished gaze followed him. He'd gone! Just like that! No goodbye, no kiss, no… nothing.

Little Joe was content, but Sabrina wasn't. As well as making love, she wanted to talk to Jonas. She wanted to feel the intimacy she'd been missing for the past several months. If their relationship before had been more about sex, at least it had a growing potential, whereas what they had now felt more like "just friends." She wanted to hear about his journey, and how the revelations he'd discovered had affected him.

Strangely enough, ever since he'd returned from what he claimed was his two-day pilgrimage with Running Bear, she felt a wall between them that hadn't been there before. A resistance to getting close to her, though he claimed he wanted to marry her.

It was strange.

Still, if Jonas Callahan thought she was going to put up with him taking catnaps in her bed and not reestablishing any of why they'd come to have little Joe in the first place, he could just take his naps elsewhere—like in the bunkhouse.

She closed her eyes, certain sleep was going to be impossible. She missed Jonas, and though she'd never expected their relationship to take a smooth path, she did want it to grow. And not just for Joe's sake. Sabrina was laying everything on the line for her big cowboy surgeon, and the waiting felt like it just might kill her.

"THIS IS TERRIBLE," FIONA SAID, hanging up the phone as Jonas walked into the kitchen the next afternoon. He had come to grab water and lunches for his brothers. Jonas wasn't worried about anything that might be vexing his sweet aunt. Whatever was bothering her now, he could fix.

After spending the night in Sabrina's bed, in the same room with his snoozing son, he felt as if the world was his. He felt he was part of a family—his own family.

"It can't be so terrible," he said serenely, giving Fiona a hug. "What's up?"

Her aunt gazed at him with big eyes. "That was Jackie on the phone. She and Darla have searched their wedding shop high and low, but the magic wedding gown is nowhere to be found. I called to check on it, but they said it isn't there."

Jonas frowned. He wasn't much for worrying with dresses and bows, certainly, but he knew how much the dress meant to Sabrina. There was a good chance she'd want to wear it when she got married, and he was hoping she'd want to get married very soon—to him. She couldn't tell him no forever, could she? He was trying to be patient, but as patience went, his was beginning to wear out. "What was it doing at the store? Didn't Seton have it last?"

"Seton took it to have some minor repairs done before reselling it. Remember, the gown has to keep moving to the next bride to keep the magic working." Fiona gave a sorrowful sigh. "I just thought I'd load the deck for the next bride in our family, just in case, not that I'm hinting or anything."

"Of course not," Jonas said, his voice sympathetic.

She shot him a wry look. "Some of the lace needed a bit of mending. Nothing serious, just the type of renovation a dress needs from time to time." Fiona blinked. "I can't imagine where it could have gotten to. It's very odd."

"Maybe Seton picked it up."

"No. Jackie and Darla said it was hanging in the back of the store for the past week, fresh from being sent off to wherever magic wedding dresses go to get fluffed up again."

Jonas shook his head. "Jackie and Darla have got so many wedding gowns, perhaps they got it confused."

"Maybe." Fiona didn't sound convinced. She looked up at him. "I suppose Sabrina would refuse to get married without the infamous gown. I mean, who could blame her?"

So *that* was what was bothering his sweet aunt. Jonas picked up his sandwiches. "That I don't know, Aunt Fiona." He didn't even want to think about the possibility of the gown that all the Callahan brides had worn going missing for good. Sabrina could probably hold out forever, if he knew her like he thought he did. "Let's just not tell her for a bit, all right? No sense in raising the alarm." *And my blood pressure. I'm positive I've just about got her on the run—running my way. We just need everything to stay quiet around here, and then I'll give Fiona the thumbs-up to plan the biggest wedding this ranch has ever seen.*

Fiona looked worried, but she peered into the lunch basket he was about to haul off. "Nothing nutritious in there. A lot of fillers, if you ask me. Bologna sandwiches, root beer, potato chips." She sniffed. "I should be put back in charge of the feeding of this crew. None of you look as good as when I was handling the feed bag. Men should never be left to feed themselves, anyway. It's an unnatural state of affairs. Like a clock running backward."

Jonas laughed. "We learned to fend for ourselves when you left. While I'll admit that mealtimes lack a certain luster without your attention, we wouldn't dream of making you take care of us, Aunt Fiona. We're capable."

"Not really," she said, a trifle indignantly. "Jonas, you're being a pill. I want my old job back."

He wasn't certain if she was up to it. He still had a lot of questions, and once they all fell back under the spell of Fiona's delicious cooking and sure handling of them, it would be a lot harder to press her.

A *lot* harder.

"I'm sure you have plenty to do to keep you busy."

"I don't." She eyed him evenly. "And I want my presidency back."

His brows rose as he fought off a smile. "Your presidency?"

"Yes." Fiona nodded. "Jonas, you can't handle the job as well as I can, admit it. The Books'n'Bingo Society is a time sink, its leadership a delicate position with many nuances. I'm sure a busy man with a new baby doesn't have time to be the captain of that bunch of hens."

"I think I've been handling my responsibilities, Aunt." He went out the door, whistling, pleased that he had Fiona in a bit of a knot. She was itching to get back in the center of things, the limelight of the ranch included. Perhaps after a few more days of her resting, he'd start letting her pick up some of her old duties.

After he was certain she'd told him everything, leaving no cards hidden in her boot.

"Jonas," Sam said, when he walked into the office

with the lunch basket. "We have something we need to talk to you about."

Jonas set the food down on the desk. "Shoot. I'm listening." He looked around at his brothers, who lounged on various old chairs, and grinned. "This grub bucket may be the last one you ever eat from that was packed by my hands."

"It can't happen too soon," Pete said. "Have we hired a service to cook for us?"

Jonas straightened. "What's that supposed to mean?"

"It means," Creed said, grabbing a bologna sandwich and a root beer, "that you may be a fine doctor, but as for cheffing the vittles, we're about to flatline around here."

"Very funny." Jonas bit into his sandwich. "None of you look like you're losing weight."

"Because we have wives who take care of us, thank heaven," Judah said. "Except for this pitiful, man-unfriendly feed bag we let you manage every day, and the odd dinner when the ladies want a break from the kitchen, we don't let you feed us. We'd starve to death."

Jonas shrugged. "Pack your own lunch boxes, you idlers."

"Okay, here's the thing." Rafe leaned to grab a sandwich, then settled back to stare at his brother. "They're talking about the lunches, and mind you, they're complaining a little. But the whining masks the real problem."

"Which is?" They just *thought* they had problems. They were all married. None of them had a woman whose bridal gown had just gone missing. He didn't even want to think how he'd tell Sabrina if it never re-appeared.

"While we applaud your style and your rich, embroidered storytelling," Sam said, "we don't think you were on a ride to solve the family mystery. And we sure as hell don't think you saw Mom and Dad."

Chapter Eleven

"In short," Sam said, continuing the theory in case Jonas didn't get what his brothers were espousing, "we think you might have hallucinated. Possibly had a major bender, after which, upon rising from a deep sleep, you recounted a very amazing, very wishful dream you'd had."

Jonas frowned. "It was real."

"Then why can't you take us there?" Judah asked. "On a mystical Diablo?"

"Because I don't know where I was." He popped the last of his sandwich into his mouth. "You have to admit I make a great bologna sandwich."

"Jonas," Creed said, interjecting reason into his tone, "you can't even tell us where you were. What direction you went in. How you got back, even." Creed gave him a serious look. "If this tale came from anyone else, we'd suggest it was time for the funhouse."

"I don't care," Jonas said. "Sabrina believes me, and that's all that matters."

"No," Pete said, his expression serious, "this time we have to know the truth. We have to know whether, in your latest quest to get away from something in your life that's troubling you, you just decided to invent a grand story for us, to satisfy all the family ghosts and skeletons. Like Dark Diablo, for instance. We know very well you bought that ranch as your escape hatch, for when you need space."

"Actually," Jonas said, "I bought it when Bode Jenkins was stirring things up, because I was afraid he might get Rancho Diablo."

"You didn't buy it then," Sam pointed out, "you only talked about it. You bought it when the case had been settled."

"True." Jonas conceded the point. "I won't deny that I've had my eye on it for some time, and that it's my dream to have my own ranch."

"Then why are you still here?" Rafe asked. "You have everything you want, don't you? Fiona's come home, not that you brought her back, even though you were supposedly searching for her. Sabrina is here, and little Joe, though we haven't heard wedding bells yet."

"Wait a minute," Jonas said, stiffening in his chair, "are you suggesting that I avoid responsibility? That I do it by creating avoidance scenarios? Stories?"

"Well—" Rafe began.

"Yes," Creed said. "Just like when we were kids, Jonas, you always had a ready ghost story to scare us, a prank when we needed fun, and a shoulder to, well, not cry on, exactly, because none of us were much for crying. But we always knew big brother supported us."

"And now you think I've cooked up a brilliant fish tale for your benefit," Jonas mused. "That's an interesting angle. You know, I might start writing crime novels. I've always wanted to write a book, and if I'm the villain you paint me as, I've certainly got the experience."

"That's not exactly what we're saying," Pete said. "Jonas, we just want you to admit that you made the whole thing up to make us feel better, to put the past to rest, so you, too, could forget that we'd never really know the truth about our parents. You don't have to keep running."

Jonas scratched his chin. "Okay. Thanks for letting me know. It's a big load off my mind." He rose, re-packed the picnic basket. "Everybody done?"

"Jonas," Sam said, "we do appreciate the effort."

"I told you, I pack a great lunch pail. Fiona's trying to take the job away from me, but I think I'm pretty much set in this saddle." He smiled as he saw the pan-icked expressions on his brothers' mugs. "You know what I mean? You just get used to some things. It be-comes part of the rhythm of your life."

"Jonas, I'm sure Fiona needs something to do," Pete said.

"Let's stay on the subject," Creed suggested. "Jonas, we're talking about our appreciation of your trying to protect us from what really happened to our parents. But we're worried about you."

"Worried about me?" He glanced around at them. "Why?"

"Because even a great storyteller like yourself shouldn't have been holed up in a back room for two days plotting your tale," Judah said. "You looked fever-ish and out of your mind when we finally found you."

"Perhaps you don't want to tell us what really hap-pened to you," Rafe said.

"Oh," Jonas said, suddenly getting it. "You think I smoked some wacky weed or something, and lost track of time, and felt like I had to cover it up with an adventure of epic proportions."

"You do like to read," Judah said. "And you have always been the big brother who did everything right, whether it was studying for medical school or becoming a brilliant doctor."

"And you think I cracked," Jonas said.

"We think you're under a lot of pressure," Pete said.

"Yeah, packing the noonday feed bag is about to kill me," Jonas said. "I'll be seeing you bunch of wienies. I think I'll go take Sabrina on a date."

He headed out of the barn, leaving his brothers to stare at one another, if they wanted, and tell themselves some more tales of Rancho Diablo. Whistling, he went to find little Joe and Sabrina. Maybe he was a little crazy, but if he was, he was crazy about a petite redhead, the one who'd come into his world as Madame Vivant, and then made him dream of turning her into Mrs. Jonas Callahan.

Life was stranger than even his brothers realized.

And he was happier than he'd been in a long time.

JONAS FOUND SABRINA packing something of her own when he found her—her suitcase. "I thought we talked about this," he said. "You stay here and Joe stays here, and we learn how to be a family."

Sabrina turned to look at him. "Jonas, listen to me. Joe and I are going back to Washington for a little while."

"Why?" Jonas asked, sitting on the bed to watch her pack. He decided he'd let her work off some of whatever was bothering her with the packing, and then when she'd calmed down a bit, he'd lure her into a good old-fashioned make-out session. "Aren't you happy here?"

"I am."

He waited for her to continue, then picked up his son from the cozy blanket nest where he was looking at his toes as if they were astonishing objects he'd never seen before. "Joe," Jonas said, "those are your toes. You've seen them a hundred times. If you want to see some different toes, I'll show you mine. They're bigger, but—"

"Jonas," Sabrina said, and he could tell she was trying to be stern with him.

"Yes, my dove?" He gave her the most innocent expression he could muster.

"Things aren't working out with me here."

"Everybody's got a complaint today," Jonas observed. "A guy takes an unscheduled road trip for two days, and the whole house turns upside down."

Sabrina glared at him. "I am not complaining, for the record, and this has nothing to do with your disappearance."

"Doesn't it?" Jonas handed Joe a plastic ring of animals to get his mind on something more educational than his toes. "You haven't been right since I returned."

"You haven't been right in a long time," Sabrina retorted.

"Have you been talking to my brothers? You shouldn't listen to them, doll. Their brains are set on Worry."

"I haven't been talking to anyone." Sabrina tossed some more things into her suitcase. "I don't need to talk to anyone. I can feel that things have changed between us."

"Not as much as I want them to," Jonas said. "And if anybody's been doing any changing, it's you."

"What do you mean?"

He smiled. "You're more beautiful, for one thing. You're sweeter, usually, when you're not trying to slink off."

"Slink off!"

"Yes." Jonas considered his little gypsy with a smile. "There was a time when I thought you were a charlatan, you know."

"I do know," Sabrina said. "And I don't need to be reminded of it, either."

"I think it weighs on you, that whole scene you and my aunt cooked up."

"It does," Sabrina admitted. "You and I got off on the wrong foot, Jonas, which is what I'm trying to tell you."

He kissed Joe's head, admired the blue romper with a yellow giraffe on the front Sabrina had put on him. Jonas's heart swelled. "This young man is going to be a heartbreaker."

Sabrina took Joe from him, keeping her this-is-serious expression on her face. "He is not going to be anything of the sort. He will always be a gentleman to ladies."

"Like dear old dad." Jonas took Joe back and waved at the suitcase. "You need two hands to pack, my love."

Sabrina gave him an uncertain look, then went on with what she'd been doing. "Anyway, I need to go clean out my apartment."

"I'll go with you," Jonas said. "I'm good at cleaning."

Sabrina shook her head. "You have too much to do here."

"All right. I'll keep little Joe while you go wrap up loose ends."

Sabrina looked like a cat that had gotten its tail stepped on. "I'm not leaving little Joe!"

"Well, you certainly can't take a baby to do the things you have to do. He'll be fine with his daddy," Jonas said, gently tweaking Joe's button nose.

"Jonas—"

"No, don't thank me. I've told you many times that I'm always available for my son. He's my best friend, aren't you?" He cradled the baby in his arms and began to leave the room. "I used to think my brothers were my best friends, but for the moment, you're much better. You're the only person in this entire house who isn't busy writing notes to leave in the Complaint Box."

Sabrina watched as Jonas headed down the stairs with her son. His son. She hesitated for a moment. There was no way she was leaving him. Yet the hunk who'd fathered him had as much of a stubborn streak as she did. If she tried to take Joe, Jonas would insist on coming with them.

It was almost as if he suspected she was trying to go back home for a while, to give her enough time to see if the two of them were really meant to be.

She jumped when Jonas's and Joe's heads poked back inside the room.

"You weren't thinking about leaving me, were you, my sweet?" Jonas asked.

"Of course not," Sabrina said.

"Because I thought I might have seen some of that

hitting-the-road-for-good sparkle in your eyes." He smiled at her, more devastatingly handsome than any man she'd ever known in her life, the only man who'd ever made her blood race and her knees threaten to buckle.

"There was no sparkle," Sabrina said.

"I didn't hear the freezing, shivering sound of arctic feet coming from you?"

"My feet are nice and toasty, thanks."

"Then bring your suitcase down to my truck, angel. The three of us are going for a ride."

"I'm not sure we want to go for a ride," Sabrina said. "I really need to go settle some things in Washington."

Jonas took her hand and led her toward the stairs. "I think we should go give Dark Diablo a second look."

Sabrina's breath caught. "Jonas—"

"I really think all the answers we're looking for are someplace other than Rancho Diablo," Jonas said, "as much as I never anticipated I'd hear those words coming from my own big mouth."

"I don't know…." The idea of spending time alone with Jonas and Joe held enormous appeal, actually. Maybe he was right. Maybe there were too many people, and not enough privacy.

"How long will we be there?" Sabrina asked. "I might need to pack more things."

Jonas glanced back at the suitcase still open on her bed. "Bring that for starters. If you need something else, we'll come get it."

She studied Jonas's face, certain he must have known she'd been planning to leave for a long time. But his expression was bland and innocent, and Sabrina decided perhaps he wasn't just trying to keep her from running off with all of her and Joe's belongings.

"We can go with you for a couple of days," Sabrina said.

"Great. Fiona!" Jonas called, as he headed down the stairs, "you're on cook patrol from now on!"

He heard clapping coming from the kitchen—Fiona, no doubt. But then he also heard whistles, and realized his brothers were grouped in there with Fiona like hungry cattle. "I see you sneaking treats to them, Aunt Fiona," he said, as Sabrina followed him. "You know they're like squirrels. If you feed them, they'll keep coming back."

"I'm not feeding them," Fiona said, but he smelled the delicious fragrance of apple tarts only Fiona could make so well. "Do you want me to pack you a small roadie basket, by chance?"

"Yes, please, Fiona," Sabrina said quickly, and his brothers burst out laughing.

"Goodbye, Jonas," Sam said. "Hope you find the real story you want to write."

His other brothers nodded. Burke grinned from his stool, munching contentedly on an apple tart.

Fiona kissed little Joe on the head. "Take good care of them, Joe," she said, "they need all the help they can get."

"Whatever," Jonas said. "You're all going to miss us when we're gone."

"Let me carry this basket for you," Creed said, picking up the hamper Fiona was tossing food into.

"I'll get a cooler," Pete said.

"I'll get a blanket," Judah said. "Planning is important when you don't have a plan."

"We have a plan," Jonas said, annoyed. "We're going to Dark Diablo."

"Ah," Pete said. "Well, bon voyage and all that rot. Sabrina, call us if you need a ride back."

"She won't," Jonas said, thinking that he'd never realized before what knuckleheads his brothers were. "I'll have my cell phone off, so don't try to call."

"A last-ditch effort to convince her," Rafe whispered, but Jonas heard him.

"No," Jonas said, "we're just escaping the asylum for a while. Come on, Sabrina."

"Not so fast," Fiona said. She took Joe from Jonas's arms. "I think this little man needs to stay here and keep Sam Bear company. And Burke. Heaven knows we don't have anything to do around here. We might as well babysit. Right, Burke?"

Smiling, he took the baby from her. "You can keep me company, Joe. I see you checked out a Lowly Worm book from the library. We'll see if we can teach you better than your father learned."

Jonas shook his head. Sabrina glanced at him and he shrugged, thinking he wouldn't mind having her to himself for a while. They had a lot to talk about, and if he was lucky, maybe other things to do, too.

They went out, and Jonas knew that no matter what happened while they were gone, he had to find a way to convince Sabrina that whatever she was afraid of, whatever reason she'd been about to leave him, what she really wanted was him.

Him and little Joe.

Chapter Twelve

Corinne, Mavis and Nadine heaved a sigh of relief. "Fortunately for us, Fiona's been too busy lately to notice what we've been up to. But she'd approve, I think," Mavis said, considering the new ad campaign that they'd planned. It was for another billboard, this one at the opposite end of town from the very successful billboard of little Joe, Sam Bear and the Callahan brothers.

"I always think of the first billboard as being of Joe and Jonas, but there are a lot of other hot guys in it," Nadine said. "None of the Callahan men are too hard on the old eye sockets."

"I know. But somehow, all I see are those sweet baby cheeks," Corinne said. "It's the whole visual, really. Man butt comes in a very sexy second."

"I don't know," Mavis said. "Every woman who's come to town since then has only mentioned the baby. It's like they think we have some secret baby-making well water to drink around here."

"It doesn't matter." Nadine stared up at the new billboard. Morning sun crested over the advertisement, and intermittent traffic rushed by on the highway outside of town, several cars slowing down to allow drivers to stare at the sign. "We've got three new families in town because of the ad. Now we need more men."

"And this should do it." Corinne gazed up at her niece, wearing a strappy wedding gown and holding little Joe. "'Do you believe in magic?'" she read from the sign. "'Diablo, home of romance,'" she finished with a flourish. "I love it."

"I still think we should have put 'Do you believe in magic? Diablo, where sexy mamas roam,'" Nadine said. "Since we're trying to bring in bachelor investors."

Corinne gazed up at the adorable picture of little Joe cradled in his mother's arms as she posed in a sexy mini wedding gown that looked a little Victoria's Secret. "If this doesn't bring the bachelors running, nothing will."

"Jonas is going to have heart failure," Nadine observed. "It's going to be a real moment of physician, heal thyself when he sees Sabrina in that barely-there wedding dress."

Corinne giggled. "Maybe it'll get Jonas moving in the right direction. I've never seen such a turtle in my life. It's like he's set on dragging this out until Christmas."

"Don't say that! Don't even put that out in the ozone!" Nadine exclaimed. "Christmas is way too late for those two to get married. If they don't get their act together soon, I'm afraid they'll never get hitched."

"Jonas is a slow-starter," Nadine said. "You're probably right."

"I don't know how Fiona deals with it," Corinne said. "But I've done my part." She gazed up at the sign with satisfaction. "If *this* doesn't put a crimp in Jonas's self-control, ladies, nothing will!"

JONAS WAS FEELING PRETTY good as he pulled out of Diablo. He'd managed to convince Sabrina to go away with him, instead of to Washington, D.C., where he was afraid he might not ever get her back. And there was no way he was going to allow his son to live several states, practically the entire country, away from him. Not when he'd barely gotten to know little Joe.

Now that he thought about it, it was a miracle he had Sabrina in his truck at all, Jonas decided. He pressed down on the accelerator, eager to put mileage between them and Rancho Diablo. If he could just get her alone, maybe they could work everything out.

And then he saw it, blooming like a white beacon at the far end of town. A new sign had gone up, one he didn't remember authorizing nor discussing. As the mayor pro tem, shouldn't that permit have come across his desk?

Jonas's heart began drumming when he realized the sign was another advertisement for Diablo—and all that white was a bride and a baby. "Do you see that?" he demanded of Sabrina.

"I think I do," she said, her voice very faint.

"It's going to have to come down at once," Jonas said. "It makes it look like this town is all about match-making. It makes it look like Diablo is just rife with single men and women looking to get married. It makes it look like we're just a bunch of hot-to-trot— Oh, no," he said, interrupting himself, staring hard as he got closer to the sign, and slowing his truck for a heart-stopping eyeful of sexily-clad Sabrina. "That's you and little Joe!"

She actually giggled. "I know."

Jonas pulled over and parked, unable to take his eyes from his beautiful red-haired lady and darling, chubby-cheeked son. He swallowed a heavy dose of emotion. "I didn't okay this."

"So?"

"There are some things I should be authorizing, and I'm pretty sure that's one of them!" Jonas realized he was a rubber stamp for the BBS—Books'n'Bingo Society—and somehow, also for the mother of his child. Every man for miles around was going to stampede into Diablo looking for the hot bride with the bountiful cleavage, sexy smile and come-hither eyes. How could a woman look so innocent and so bedroom-worthy all at once? He tore his gaze away from the expanse of Sabrina's legs on full display, and faced the object of his heartfelt…jealousy. "That's going to have to come down."

"I don't think so," Sabrina said serenely. "It's getting lots of attention, and that's what Diablo wants. Everyone loves a baby, you know." She smiled again, apparently unaware of how she was tearing him up. "Do you see that Joe is wearing a T-shirt matching the one he wore for your shoot? Only this time it says Hot Stuff." She smiled at him. "The BBS wanted his shirt to read *My Mama's A Cowgirl* because your shirt said *Cowboys Do It Better,* but I told them I wasn't a cowgirl. I believe in truth in advertising."

Jonas blinked. There was definitely too much truth in advertising on that billboard. Joe's Hot Stuff proclamation was entirely too close to his mother's generous cleavage. He swallowed tightly. "Sabrina, it's coming down."

"It's not." She shook her head. "Don't be a chauvinist."

"I'm not." How could he make her understand? There had to be ten cars parked under the sign, probably gawking, horny men. And it was before noon! By the time he'd gotten Sabrina convinced and packed to come with him—and assured that Joe would be fine without her—early morning light was breaking over the town. "I'm being practical. That sign is dangerous."

"And yours isn't?"

"No. It's altogether different."

"Jonas," Sabrina said, "I'm not a child you can order around."

He heard mulishness and perhaps a tinge of annoyance, and realized that although he might be about to win a battle, he was about to cede a war. Jonas sighed, realizing he'd been bested fair and square, once again, by the ladies of the town. "Could we compromise and have you wearing something less cataclysmically hot?" Jonas mopped at his brow. "I'm pretty sure it's already a hundred degrees, and it's not even eleven o'clock."

"No," Sabrina said, "you'll hurt Corinne's feelings. And Nadine's, and Mavis's. They worked very hard on this."

"I'll just bet they did." They'd worked superhard on giving him a coronary *and* an erection. He was pretty certain either one might kill him sooner than he wanted to expire. Jonas sighed again and started the truck. "Sometimes I feel that for a mayor and president of a busybody society, a lot of decisions are made without my approval. Deliberately."

When Sabrina didn't reply, he glanced over at her. She was smiling at him, and laughing a little, and Jonas shook his head.

If they were trying to kill him, they were probably going to succeed.

But he was just that much more determined to get a *yes* out of his hot Diablo poster girl.

"HOME SWEET HOME," Jonas said an hour and a half later, pulling into Tempest, and then making the turn on the dirt road to Dark Diablo.

"I wouldn't necessarily call it that," Sabrina said, looking at the small farmhouse.

"It'll grow on you." Jonas got out of the truck, went around to open her door. "Come on, wild thing. I need to see if I left a beer in the fridge."

"Still worked up?" Sabrina asked as he gathered her into his arms and carried her over the threshold.

"You have no idea." He breathed in Sabrina's scent and sighed to himself. *This* was home. The woman he held in his arms was his home, if he could only convince her of it. "Listen, I had the strangest feeling that you were trying to leave me last night. I just wanted to check in with you about that probably incorrect hunch I had."

"Your hunch was right on," Sabrina said, staring into his eyes. "In fact, you'd find a plane ticket in my purse if you looked."

He gulped painfully. "Why?"

"I don't know." Sabrina hugged herself, staring at

him with big eyes. "Maybe you're not the only one with a journey to take, Jonas."

That didn't sound good. He didn't want Sabrina on a journey without him. Something told him they'd already spent plenty of time apart, in their own separate worlds. It seemed to him the next trip either of them took should be together. "I'll take you anywhere you want to go, babe."

She hesitated, then turned to glance around. "The house looks different."

He couldn't help grinning as he set her down in the hallway. "I made note of your reservations and called in some help."

She walked into the kitchen and he followed. "It's charming," Sabrina said. "New fixtures, even."

"The latest in kitchen doodads," Jonas said proudly. "The whole house has been updated to look as much like Rancho Diablo as possible, on a much smaller scale, of course." He led her up the stairs. "New paint, and even a nursery."

"Goodness." Sabrina looked at the dark brown crib and matching rocking chair. "You've been busy."

"The credit for all the updating goes to some kind ladies in Tempest who worked quickly and efficiently from pictures I sent from my phone." Judging by the expression on Sabrina's face, which was far less horrified than when she'd first seen Rancho Diablo, the ladies had acquitted themselves well. "They were worth every penny, in my less than experienced opinion."

"I'll say they were." Sabrina wandered into the master bedroom. "If I didn't know better, I'd think this was a new bed."

"Everything's new." Jonas sat on the mattress, bouncing a little, testing it. "Everything but the outside of the house is new. I left that for later. It needs a roof and some new guttering. None of the fun stuff. So I left it."

"Who picked out the colors for this room?"

He watched Sabrina check out the objects d'art and sturdy, dark mahogany furniture. He hoped she liked everything he'd done. If not, well, he had a plan B. "I picked out everything for every room, believe it or not. There's a lady in town who's had a shop forever. She knows everybody in the business. I told her the style of house I wanted—pretty much like Rancho Diablo— sent her some pictures, and she uploaded whatever she found that she thought I might like. Decorating over the internet is easier than it sounds," he said.

"Ugh," Sabrina said. "I'm glad you had fun. Decorating isn't exactly my thing."

"Listen, Sabrina," Jonas said, pulling her to him and relaxing onto the bed with her, as much as she was willing to relax around him. "This is all window dressing. I don't care about any of it. If you didn't like it, I'd send it all back and never think twice about it. All I care about is you and little Joe."

She gazed at him with those big eyes he loved. "Are you turning into a romantic, Jonas?"

"Whatever it takes, love." He kissed her hand, then her fingertips. "Is it working?"

"It might be," Sabrina said. "Keep talking."

"Nope," Jonas said. "If I'm scoring points, I'd better quit while I'm ahead and let my mouth do better things." He kissed her, closing his eyes to enjoy the sweet softness of her mouth, and it was like they'd never been apart for more than a day. "God," he said huskily, gazing down into her eyes as she lay back on the bed, "I remember everything about you, Sabrina. Only it's better now."

"Better?" Sabrina stared up at him. "How can it be better?"

"Because now I know how much I want it. I never want to lose you again." Jonas kissed her more deeply, losing himself in the magic that was Sabrina. "I thought I'd lost you forever."

"Oh, Jonas." She stared up at him. "Let's not talk about anything that happened before. Let's just think about being together now."

He hoped that was the invitation it sounded like. So far, matters were going pretty well. She hadn't leaped back into the truck as she practically had upon seeing Dark Diablo the first time. She seemed a lot warmer to him. Jonas figured maybe he was finally doing something right.

"Whatever you want, babe," he said. He ran a palm down her arm, then down her side, aching to touch her. She looked so pretty in her blue flowered sundress. He'd never wanted anything so badly in his life as he wanted her—but he wasn't about to muck up the big moment by rushing things. "Hey, I've had the fridge stocked," Jonas said. "Are you hungry? Because if you are, I can whip up some—"

"Be quiet, Jonas," Sabrina said, and pulled him to her. She kissed him this time, and Jonas's racing heart stilled, almost stopping in his chest. This was different. This was Sabrina wanting him, pursuing him in a way he couldn't mistake. He'd waited so long for her to want him that he hung back, his blood pounding with wild hope—and when she traced his chest with one light hand and began undoing his shirt buttons with nimble fingers, Jonas knew all his dreams were about to come true.

"Sabrina," he murmured, and she said, "Shh," so he hushed and let his lips and hands do his communicating. She arched under his fingers, moaning, and it was as if he'd never lost her, only better, because now he knew how precious she was. He kissed her and loved her and held her tight, and when she pulled at his belt buckle, he undressed her slowly, kissing her body the way he'd wanted to all the months they'd been apart. When he had her naked to his hungry eyes, Jonas laid her in the soft, freshly washed sheets of his new bed, stripped off his jeans and the rest of his clothes, and made love to her as he never had before.

"Don't stop," she told him, and he didn't, because he didn't want to, never had wanted to. He wasn't about to stop until they both passed out from exhaustion. Her skin was like satin, her body made for his, and when she finally cried out in his arms, he held her tight, rocked by his own feelings, which were somehow her feelings, too. And Jonas thought he'd never been so happy in his entire life.

All he could think when Sabrina fell asleep in his arms was, *nothing is ever going to take this away from me again.*

Nothing.

Chapter Thirteen

Sabrina and Jonas had been at Dark Diablo for only two days when the romantic interlude took a typical turn. All the Callahans pulled up, in five trucks and the family van, and Sabrina stared out with a grin at the melee of people getting out of vehicles. "Now I know why the idea of Dark Diablo attracts you so much. The Callahans are a big bunch when they're all together in one place."

"Tell me about it."

She followed Jonas out onto the porch, hoping little Joe was among the crowd. When she spied her son in Fiona's arms, she hurried over to snatch him to her for an enthusiastic kiss. "Joe! I've been missing you!"

"I figured as much." Fiona beamed. "He's the best baby. All the Callahan babies are good."

"Most of the time," Sam said, lugging his three girls to the front door. "Jonas, this is some spread. How come you've never invited us out here before?"

Jonas scowled. "I didn't invite you now."

"True." Sam laughed. "But don't tell the girls. It was their idea, and they said you told them they had an open invitation. It's so hot outside they want to swim in that creek of yours you're always bragging about."

"That sounds like fun!" Sabrina hurried to find her sister and thc Callahan wives. "A swimming party! Joe's first swim!"

Seton glanced at her as she took Sam Bear from his car seat. "We weren't sure if you were ready for a break or not. So we figured a few hours of family might be a welcome intervention."

"It's all been fine." Sabrina smiled. "It's like we were never apart. In fact, it's almost as if we're rediscovering each other."

"That's great. And you do look happy." Seton hugged her. "So, are there wedding bells?"

"I don't know about that," Sabrina said, hoping no one had overheard the question. "We're taking things one step at a time."

"Good plan." Seton handed her a small, striped diaper bag. "That's got little Joe's swimsuit in it."

"He doesn't have a swimsuit."

"He does now, because Aunt Seton went shopping. I got one with tiny bears on it for Sam Bear, and one with tiny frogs on it for Joe. I thought they were so cute! Little-men bathing suits," Seton said. "I'm afraid my swim bottoms are much bigger than their trunks."

"Yes, well, we've all changed a little." Sabrina pulled out the suit and smiled at the frogs. "This is hysterical. Thank you, Seton. I can't wait to see it on Joe!" She hurried off to try the trunks on her baby, suddenly realizing she'd never seen Jonas wearing a swimsuit. She wondered if he'd swim or just stand cn the creek bank barking commands and playing big bad lifeguard.

To her shock, Jonas took Joe from her—and the froggy swimsuit—and dressed him in it. "Hold still, son, you tiny Adonis," he said, snapping a photo with his phone. "This is going up on the new Callahan family website."

"Oh," Sabrina said, suddenly realizing what he was up to. "That's a great idea."

"Makes me wonder why I never thought of it before." He laughed at Joe in his plump trunks over the water-proof diaper. "No need for sending pictures by carrier pigeon."

"Your parents will be able to see everything as the children grow. They'll barely miss a thing—and no one will ever know." Sabrina looked at Jonas, knowing how much he'd changed since his visit to his parents. It was as if he was thinking of the past, present and future now, planning each step with precision. "It's a great idea."

"Well, I have great inspiration." He picked his son up off the bed and blew a raspberry on his tummy. "Let's go swim, son. I've had a couple of tire swings hung over the deep part. We'll see if your uncles still remember how to swing. Probably not, I'm guessing. We'll have to teach them. They don't realize this, but I'm the king of the creek when it comes to tire swinging, and I fully expect that you'll follow in my footsteps."

"Jonas," Sabrina said, hurrying after the big cowboy. Jonas was the sexiest thing she'd ever laid eyes on in his black trunks, holding little Joe in his froggy trunks. She hoped Fiona didn't realize that the *Cowboys Do It Better* billboard on the outskirts of town would be ever so much sexier with Jonas half-naked, wearing only swim trunks. "That'd be a traffic jam," she muttered.

"Did you say something, my dove?" Jonas asked,

tossing her a striped beach towel. "I hope you brought a suit, Sabrina. Otherwise, you may be the first Callahan female in the buff in my creek."

"I don't think that'll happen," she said, rolling her eyes, fully intending to rescue her son from his father's adventurous plans.

"You don't think you have a suit? Never mind. There's a cute one upstairs in the bureau. Seton picked it out, so don't blame it on me."

"No, I meant— Never mind." Sabrina followed Jonas, although she was dying to get into the suit and play with her family. "Jonas, I don't think I want Joe on a tire swing."

He turned to look at her with a smile. "You're going to be one of those protective mothers, I can tell."

"Well, yes," she said. "Of course I'll be protective."

"So sweet," he said, kissing her hand. "In the meantime, I'll protect you, although I warn you, there are some things beyond my control."

"I don't need protecting," Sabrina said. "Jonas, what are you talking about?"

He smiled, his eyes twinkling with mischief. Then she heard it: loud whooping laughter rushing toward them. She froze as Jonas watched benignly. "Don't say I didn't tell you there was a suit for you upstairs," he said, seconds before she was scooped up, like all the other Callahan women, in the arms of a Callahan cowboy.

She was carried to the dock by Sam, though with Seton riding on his back, hamstringing his progress, he was a bit slower than the other brothers. Still, Sam was big enough to make good time to the creek. They went off the edge, and a second before she hit the water,

Sabrina squealed, loving being treated like part of the family.

She came up for air and glanced around at all the Callahan brides in the water with her and their husbands. "Jonas," Sabrina called, "do I have to come out there and get you?"

He handed little Joe to Fiona, who was standing with Burke and Corinne, watching with the Callahan children as they stared at their parents splashing in the week. The kids who could walk were equipped with floaties and inflatable rings, and Sabrina wished she had a picture of everyone together, celebrating that all the bad times were far behind them at last. Jonas cannonballed in next to her and Sabrina let out the obligatory squeal, thinking she'd never been so happy.

Maybe this time everything would be different.

FOUR HOURS LATER, the Rancho Diablo group left Dark Diablo and headed back home, with happy children napping and lightly sunned, and adults satisfied that they'd surprised Sabrina and Jonas with their visit.

"You know they were checking up on us," Sabrina said.

"Actually, I think they saw themselves as the cavalry." Jonas grinned at her. "If you wanted a ride back, you just missed it, lady."

She gave him an arch look. "You get one more day, cowboy."

"I can do a lot with twenty-four hours, trust me."

She dangled from one of the tire swings, enjoying watching the sun setting over Dark Diablo, loving how it highlighted Jonas against the backdrop of the house in the distance. "Do you realize there are eighteen children at Rancho Diablo now, if you count Diane and Sidney's three?"

"Which we do," Jonas said. "Don't ever let Creed hear you say that they might not be part of the head count. His small wizened brain would explode. As far as he's concerned, he has five children, some of which he just happens to share with his new buddy Sidney." Jonas laughed. "Creed thinks he won the race for biggest family, and it's not about the race for the ranch, either. He's crazy about those kids."

Sabrina wiggled her toes and wondered if she should drag Jonas in for a twilight swim in the creek. "I guess Fiona's plan, which she hired me to kick-start, has succeeded with gold stars and giant belt buckles."

"Not really." Jonas glowered at her. "We have Pete's poppets, Fiona, Molly and Elizabeth, Creed's crew, Joy Patrice, Grace Marie, Ashley, Suzanne and Lincoln Rose, Judah's kinder, Jennifer Belle and Molly Mavis, Rafe's gang Janet, Julianne and Judith, Sam's squad of Sam Bear, Sharon Marie, Devon Bridget and tiny Sarah Colleen, and I notice you're counting little Joe in the eighteen. However, may I remind you that of all Callahan children, only one of them doesn't bear the Callahan name? Mine? As far as I'm concerned, you've fallen down on your assignment, beautiful."

Sabrina didn't know what to say about that, so she dived into the water, not surprised when Jonas joined her.

"Are you softening toward Dark Diablo?" he asked, tugging her close. She still had on the shorts and

T-shirt she'd been wearing when Sam tossed her in the creek, so Jonas merely grabbed a belt loop and pulled her toward him.

"It's very picturesque here." Sabrina flicked water in his face and paddled away. "But I still wouldn't want to live here. I'd want to be at Rancho Diablo with the family."

"Those busybodies? You see how they'll always be in your business. You couldn't even leave for a small three-day vacation without them riding to the rescue."

Sabrina grabbed a float one of the kids had left behind, and rested on it. "I knew they were coming."

Jonas's handsome face registered surprise. "You did?"

"Yes. Seton told me before we left that you'd promised everyone a family vacation, the first entire family vacation, out here at Dark Diablo. It wasn't really a vacation, more like an outing, but the ladies were looking forward to it. Plus, Fiona understood that I couldn't live without seeing little Joe for more than a couple of days."

"You little sneaker." Jonas playfully dunked her under water and reeled her in once again. "You could have shared that information."

"I could have, but I didn't." Sabrina kissed him on the mouth, a fast one, and Jonas's eyes turned dark sapphire.

"Are you starting something?" he asked.

"I might be," Sabrina said. "How are you for skinny-dipping?"

His expression was priceless before it turned distinctly predatory. "Come here, gypsy. I can have you undressed so fast it'll make you happy."

Laughing, she tossed her shirt at him. "I can take care of myself. You just get your snorkel ready."

"That's my girl," Jonas said, and tossed his trunks on the bank.

FOR ONCE THE PLACE was completely empty and silent. He couldn't remember a time when Rancho Diablo was as deserted as the Old West. The old lady had been at it again, stringing her infernal lights—this time for the Fourth of July, he guessed—because everything was in red, white and blue. He thought it was one of the more annoying things about this place, the old lady's constant Happyland decorating.

In his world, twinkling lights and a joyous spirit were unknown.

Sonny went inside the main house, careful not to leave any fingerprints, although the Callahans knew of his existence. He didn't care. It was good for them to know that he was waiting. One day they'd slip up, and he'd find their parents and turn them over to the cartel. A job like this took years to complete, and he was patient.

He dug through the old woman's recipe box—nothing but recipes—and eyed a section of the wall that caught his attention. Then he realized that the wallpaper hid a lock in one of the patterns, so he picked that easily, finding a gun cabinet that he eyed with regret before closing the hidden panel again. The Callahans were well-armed, considering that they rarely, if ever, hunted. Thousands of dollars' worth of shotguns and hunting rifles were in the case, wasted, in his opinion, since they were never used.

Suddenly, Sonny thought he'd seen a shadow cross the window in the kitchen. He hesitated, waiting, watching.

After a moment, he realized it must have been a cloud momentarily blocking the sun, or a bird flying past. He went on with his search.

Somewhere in this house were the answers he sought. Nobody disappeared completely without leaving some trace behind. A photo with an address on the back, a coded address kept in a safe place or a toy with a special message written on it, to remind children of a family's love. He'd found the information he needed in a variety of places over the years on other jobs he'd worked and he always found his target, eventually. This was the grown-up version of hide-and-seek, and he enjoyed the thrill of the hunt, because the prize was life... or death.

With stakes that high, the game was always very rewarding for the winner.

He went down into the basement, though he'd checked there before. The long scar in the floor caught his attention; it always made him think someone was buried here. Something *was* buried there, but it was probably just pipe. There was no telling what the crazy old woman might put in her basement. It creeped the hell out of him, and he didn't scare easily.

He kicked at the dirt, scraping off a few inches. After a moment, he left the tamped-down, footlockershaped patch of dirt alone. Any clues he was searching for weren't in the ground—the old woman just wasn't smart enough to cover her tracks by burying any pertinent evidence.

After a last long, hard look at the floor, Sonny left, knowing time was on his side.

Chapter Fourteen

It had been a wonderful vacation with Jonas. Sabrina was well aware that he'd meant their time together to be a mini-honeymoon of sorts. She looked at the big man as he packed the truck, and wished things could be different. But she knew it couldn't. As much as she loved him, as much as he loved her, and though they both loved little Joe like mad, she was never going to be able to say yes to Jonas.

The die had been cast from the beginning, when she'd accepted the job from Fiona.

"Jonas," Sabrina said, going to the truck.

"Yes," he said, ceasing his packing to give her a smile. "I do, in fact, have time for a quickie. Or a full afternoon, if you prefer, of uninterrupted, last-chance lovemaking."

She smiled, wishing she could take him up on the sexy offer. Since they'd spent a great portion of the past three days undressed and in each other's arms, there was nothing she'd love to do more than enjoy an encore. "I need to talk to you."

"I'm listening, although I will say that I listen even better when you're naked in my arms."

"You do not." Sabrina shook her head. "I may have

your full attention when I'm naked, but listening isn't what you're doing."

"Sure it is. I listen for all the right sounds to come from my beautiful lady. Then I know all is well in my world."

She seated herself on the open truck gate. "Jonas, I'm going back to D.C."

He looked at her, waiting.

"I have no choice," she said, feeling miserable. "I don't belong here, as much as I want to be at Rancho Diablo. Or Dark Diablo. Or anywhere with you."

He blinked. "Sabrina, you know I'd marry you as soon as you said the word. Just say it."

"It's not about that. Believe me, I'm tempted, if for no other reason than for Joe's sake. Don't you think it would mean a lot to me—everything—for him to be a Callahan?"

Jonas's heart seemed to crumple. He could tell by Sabrina's tone—by her expression—that this conversation had been a long time in coming. Somehow he knew that she'd been waiting, holding in a confession, until it felt like a dam that was about to burst.

He picked her up from the gate and carried her to the house, seating her on the recently installed porch swing. "Say whatever's on your mind, babe."

She took a breath to steady herself, choose her words. Jonas waited, his heart thundering.

"Did you ever wonder how I could go this long without working, Jonas?"

"I thought you said you were on an extended maternity leave."

"Jonas," she said softly, "little Joe is seven months old, soon to be eight."

Okay, so he hadn't examined the particulars of her bank account and job status. "Sabrina, if this is about money, I have every intention of taking care of you and Joe."

Sabrina didn't speak for a long moment. Then she said, "Jonas, your aunt has been paying me from the start."

"Okay. I don't care. It's just not important to me, Sabrina." He shrugged. "She hired you to pull a gag, you did your job admirably, as we recently discussed, and it's not like you don't do plenty around here for her and for us. I thought she had you being her personal assistant for a while, anyway."

"She left for months," Sabrina said. "But I was still working for her."

He didn't know where this was going, but it seemed to bother Sabrina, so he waited for her to finish her story. "Oh, I get it. You're trying to tell me that Fiona still has you spying on us, reporting in when she's not around. Like Chelsea did."

"Before I went to Washington, your aunt asked me to stay and work here. She said she needed someone to keep an eye on things, especially since she planned to be leaving for an extended time. She wanted me to look out for anything that looked suspicious, but mainly, she said she wanted me to keep you busy."

"Keep me busy?" Jonas blinked.

Sabrina nodded. "Fiona was afraid you'd start looking for your parents if you didn't have something else to keep you occupied."

Jonas frowned. "You made love to me so I wouldn't look for our parents?"

"No." A blush crossed Sabrina's cheeks. "That wasn't in the job description, Jonas."

"I don't care how you ended up here, just so long as you stay permanently in my bed," Jonas said. "I couldn't care less how you got there."

"Jonas," Sabrina said, "I don't feel good about being someone your aunt hired to sidetrack you."

"Don't worry about it, sweetheart." He scooped her into his lap. "You did keep me out of trouble. Believe me, I'll kiss Fiona the first chance I get for finding me such a red-hot lady. I'm just fine with how her scheme turned out."

"Jonas." Sabrina got out of his lap and sat next to him. "I can't do it. I can't be the woman who ensnared you."

"Why? I'm not complaining. I like being snared. Every man wants to know that a woman set her cap for him."

That was exactly how he felt. He always enjoyed knowing that he had a special place in Sabrina's heart. He liked her being a bit of a wild child. The fact that she'd thought she was putting one over on him entertained him immensely. He liked smart women, and Sabrina was intelligent as well as sexy. "Hey, I've got an idea. Why don't you think up another plan, the kind where we decide you want to trick me into marrying you? You could get me tipsy, or we could go to Vegas and pretend we are strangers who meet and get married by an Elvis impersonator—"

Sabrina stood up. "Jonas, a marriage that starts with a falsehood ends with regret."

"We're not ending anything, gorgeous. Come sit back in my lap. I think you've got me excited with all this talk of your bad-girl side. I want to try out this porch swing and see if you can keep your balance as good as those circus performers you used to hang around with."

"Jonas!" Sabrina stamped her foot. "You said you'd listen, and you're not."

"Which is pretty much what your job was supposed to be, wasn't it? To keep me busy?"

She put her hands on her hips. "Look, Dr. Goodlove, I can't marry someone I was hired to lie to."

Jonas shrugged. "I could have fallen for anyone else in the world. There was no guarantee I'd fall for you. As a matter of fact, if you'd been in a lineup of hot chicks, you're probably not the one I would have chosen at first glance."

"Oh, really?"

He smiled when he heard the annoyance in her tone. "I'm pretty sure not. Pistol-hot and well-endowed, yet petite redheads were never my thing before. I used to have a real thing for tall blondes who could barrel race. I haven't seen you racing around anything but cacti, chasing little Joe. So I wouldn't worry anymore about all this guilt you've been holding in, doll. I'm good with your naughty side. I'm pretty sure you complete me."

"Because you're so good and all."

"Yep," he said. "Now let's see if we can rock this porch swing."

"Jonas," Sabrina said, "I was staying with Bode Jenkins so I could spy on you."

"It's okay," Jonas insisted, "though I personally wouldn't have subjected you to that hell when you could have kept tabs on me from my own bed. Wouldn't that have been easier?"

"I was trying not to fall for you, you ape," Sabrina said, getting testy, something she did from time to time, always managing to amuse him. "Besides which, I liked Mr. Jenkins, even though you didn't. And Fiona said it was a great idea to go over there, because I could keep an eye on him."

"True," Jonas said. "As long as you were still thinking about me, that's fine."

"So I was privy to a lot that was going on that you never knew about, from the other side of the fence, so to speak. The only reason he had the lawsuit going as long as he did was because it kept all you men at Rancho Diablo."

Jonas stopped ogling Sabrina's cleavage, his attention caught by what she was saying. "What are you talking about?"

Sabrina seated herself on the porch near him. "You were in Dallas, some of the Callahans were rodeoing…" Sabrina shrugged. "He and Fiona were in cahoots."

Jonas blinked. "You're trying to tell me that all the stories Fiona told us were poppycock?" He gave Sabrina's face, miserable with her confession, a searching look. "You've believed one too many of someone's tales, love. Bode is not a silent, long-suffering angel on our behalf, and if Fiona wanted us home to stay, why didn't she just say so instead of concocting an expensive lawsuit?"

"If she'd said please come home, would any of you have done so?" Sabrina gazed at him. "You had a successful practice. Other brothers were working off wild oats. Who would have come home, Jonas?"

No one. It was true.

"Why?"

"Because of the mercenary in the canyons. And not just him, but the rest of what Fiona feared might come. The story about losing the ranch wasn't one she just made up. She genuinely feared that someone was going to get killed—one of her nephews."

"So us being at Rancho Diablo was safer?"

"Do you remember when someone shot at Creed when he was getting married?"

"Yeah. A hunter's gun, or something else, misfired."

Sabrina didn't say anything. Jonas looked at her, trying to understand. "You're telling me that all those coincidences and accidents we tried to lay at Bode's door were never Bode. It was someone else."

"Someone much worse. Fiona was terrified. She had no one to trust but Burke."

"And Bode…and you, apparently."

"Bode believed his wife would have wanted him to help you boys. That was his motivation. Did you ever stop and wonder what he would have done with a ranch the size of Rancho Diablo?"

"I did. It didn't make sense at the time." Jonas thought over the past years of heartbreak and misery they'd blamed on Bode. "I'm just having trouble believing that he was some kind of altruistic, avenging saint looking out for us."

"He had to be the bad guy, so you men would keep fighting for your home. And he was angry with the Callahans because he'd lost his wife, and he blamed your parents. Over time, of course, when Rafe married Julie, Bode changed. When he found himself the grandfather of three adorable little girls, he softened. But in the beginning, if he hadn't been so formidable, none of you would have stayed to protect Fiona. That was what was uppermost in all your minds, and she used that to her advantage." Sabrina looked at him. "I remember the night I met you, how angry you were because you thought I was some kind of gypsy trying to take advantage of your little aunt."

"I was a bit riled," Jonas said, remembering. He gazed at Sabrina, shaking his head. "I even followed the circus train out of town, determined to give you what-for if you'd robbed the house or done anything to hurt Fiona."

Sabrina nodded. "I know. She told me."

"There are no secrets at Rancho Diablo."

A small smile crept onto Sabrina's face. "I liked the fact that you were so protective of her. It was one of the first things that made me start falling for you."

He was trying to process everything he was hearing. His mind was whirling, reeling. Part of him wanted to deny what Sabrina was telling him; the logic that had gotten him through med school and made him a good surgeon was trying to find a hole in her story. But what was icing his brain and freezing his heart to the point he could barely think was that he thought he heard Sabrina trying to tell him that she wasn't in love with him—because he'd only been a *job* to her. One of Fiona's escapades. "Why wouldn't she just have told us about Sonny? Wouldn't it have been a lot safer for us if we'd known what to look out for, protect ourselves against?"

Sabrina shrugged. "She said she couldn't tell you. Fiona said that if you suspected, if any of you knew that he was down there, you'd kill him."

"Hell, yeah," Jonas said. "That's a given."

"Exactly. And then whoever'd sent him would send someone else. Fiona said that since she and Burke knew about him, and he didn't know they were aware of him, it was better to deal with the devil they knew than a new one. To be honest, Fiona wasn't that afraid of Sonny. She was more afraid of getting run off the ranch. To stay here, to keep it the way it had been when your parents were here, she needed all of you here to safeguard it. She said there was strength in numbers. And the way to keep men buzzing around the hive, she said, was to provide lots of honey."

Jonas laughed in spite of himself. "She's crazy. But absolutely right. Her plan certainly worked on my brothers." But it wasn't working for him. And he had a big reason he needed everything to go his way—Joe. Jonas shot Sabrina a disgruntled look. "Is there a reason why, out of all of us, I got the one woman who isn't in the mood to settle down?"

"It's just hard, Jonas. See it from my perspective."

"I can't. I have Joe to think about."

"But you didn't know that before. And you were all set to marry Chelsea."

"Because I didn't know!" Jonas glowered at Sabrina.

"Fiona's not the only one capable of subterfuge," she observed.

"My fake engagement was just to save face. You know that."

"I do. And you'll have to understand that I would never have come back if Seton and Sam hadn't conspired to bring me home."

Jonas straightened. "I still have a bone to pick with you about that. Were you never going to tell me about Joe?"

Sabrina looked at him, her expression torn. "I wanted to. I wanted you to be part of his life. I just didn't know what life there was going to be at Rancho Diablo. Everything was crazy. And you seemed like you were just in it for the sexual adventure, the doctor having his fling. Opposites attract, but they don't fall in lasting love stuff."

"Well, you overthought that." Jonas was getting a bit steamed. "You're supposed to be clairvoyant, aren't you? You couldn't tell that I was crazy about you?"

Sabrina shook her head. "You never asked me out, never did anything but visit my bed. When I found out I was pregnant with Joe, all I could think of was that I didn't want you if I'd had to catch you that way. What did you call it? Setting my cap?" Her expression was strained. "It wouldn't have lasted that way, Jonas."

"But still," he said, "that's all in the past. You can't not agree to marry me just because of a bunch of little misunderstandings."

Sabrina stood, her posture stiff and resolute. "Jonas,

I do love you. I'm madly in love with you. But we're too different. I can't marry you."

He stared up at her, realizing her mind was made up. "Sabrina—"

"I'm so sorry," she said, her voice soft. "Jonas, we built a foundation on sand that shifts constantly. I was brought in by your aunt. I kept the family secrets. But never did I plan on having a baby or falling for you. In my heart, I always knew your attraction to me was only sexual, and at the time, I was okay with that."

He saw tears sparkling in Sabrina's eyes. Horrified, he realized she was basically telling him it was over between them. She believed every word she was saying, had no idea how much he loved her. Voicing the words wouldn't change anything now. There was little he could do but stand helplessly, knowing that the woman he loved had looked squarely at her life and realized that what was in her heart wasn't strong enough to overcome the obstacles in their path.

She took his hand, as she would with any good friend. He didn't know how he could change her mind, explain that she was his heart and soul, his whole world now, with little Joe. In silence they walked to the truck. There was nothing else left to say, and Jonas didn't think he'd ever hurt this much, not since his parents had left. The pain was swift and fierce, but he knew Sabrina's independent heart was one of the things he loved most about her.

So he had to let her go, even if he could practically hear his own heart shattering.

Chapter Fifteen

The family meeting was held in the upstairs library a few days later, on schedule, just like always. Except Jonas felt as if everything was out of order, out of sync. He was pretty sure he was dying inside. He'd come so far, conquered the demons he needed to conquer, only to realize in the end that he still hadn't won Sabrina.

It was a killer.

"So you're just going to let her leave?" Sam asked, agog.

His brothers all stared at him with dismayed expressions. "There's nothing I can do," Jonas said. "Sabrina is a strong, independent woman who knows her own mind. What am I supposed to do? Beg? Plead?" He shook his head. "The problems are twofold. Sabrina couldn't make the transition from employee to family member, and she doesn't believe I'm in love with her, no matter how many times I ask her to marry me."

Pete shook his head. "That doesn't make sense. The BBS put her in that bride getup on a billboard right on the edge of Diablo, to lure in new residents and customers. Would they do that with someone they didn't consider a daughter of this town?"

"Not to mention how much you do love her," Creed said, "and I'm certain you told her that often."

"She's Corinne's niece," Judah said. "Of course she belongs here. More importantly, she's little Joe's mother. She's an equal part of this family."

"And you love her madly," Creed repeated, "which I'm sure you told her often. Didn't you, Jonas?"

"I'm sure I did," Jonas said, realizing his ham-headed brother was trying to make a point. "Anyway, I'm not exactly just letting her and little Joe leave. I'm going with them." Jonas raised his glass to his brothers. "She doesn't know it yet, but if the mountain won't go to Moses, Moses will just have to go to the mountain. Or whatever."

Rafe rolled his eyes. "I applaud the plan, if not the mangling of the expression. Look, I'll fly you guys up there. You'll need help packing her up, and by the time I take a few scenic detours around the country, you'll have talked her into staying in Diablo and marrying you, the last of the lovesick cowboys."

"And I'm positive you told Sabrina every single day that she wasn't just a hot, sexy babe in your bed you knocked up, but that you love her madly," Creed stated, digging at his brother.

Jonas jumped to his feet. "I can't remember if I actually said the words! Does it matter? I do love her, I always have, but I can't change the way she feels about all her own little ghosts and fears!"

"Oh, brother," Creed said. "Didn't we always say that when it was Jonas's turn to get a woman to the altar, there was going to be all kinds of wailing and gnashing of teeth?"

Sam nodded. "I do believe there was a consensus that when Jonas fell, it was going to be uglier than all of us combined."

Jonas sank into his chair. "Okay, advice column enthusiasts, what do you suggest I do differently? Because I can't make my own heart stop beating like Big Ben. I can't make it slow down or make it quit racing. I feel like it's going to implode."

They all looked at him with pitying expressions.

"It's a terrible thing to see a grown man cry," Sam said.

"I'm not crying," Jonas snapped. "But you're going to be in a minute if you don't stop spouting nonsense."

Pete had been quiet during this boisterous baking of his brother, but now he stood. "Jonas, you're going to have to stop thinking with that oversize Ivy League brain of yours and get emotional."

Jonas glanced up from the sofa he'd slumped into. "Emotional? Like you lot of rinky-dink Romeos?"

"Exactly like us," Creed said. "You've got to sweep her off her feet. Sabrina's a sexy girl, if you haven't noticed—"

"Thanks, I think I have," Jonas said dryly.

"And she has emotions like every other female. If you just try to think outside the box, you may find that female-psyche component of yourself, which is key at this time," Creed finished.

"What he's trying to say," Judah said, "is that you haven't bought flowers, or a ring, or said you loved her, bro. Just because you can't keep your hands off of her does not compute to love to Sabrina. *Capiche?*"

"It's true," Rafe agreed. "Just because she might be

a touch clairvoyant doesn't mean she can read your mind on how you feel about her. And feel free to reassure your jingling little gypsy that we've all long ago forgiven her for being in on the plot to see us tied down. In fact, we hold Sabrina in the highest regard. We're all exuberantly happy with our wives and families. You're the only one who's sad. You might point that out to her."

"You've figured out everything else, Jonas," Sam said. "You can figure out how to fix this, too."

"Okay," he said, feeling better now that he sensed his brothers were totally on his side and didn't think he was a big dumb gorilla who'd loused things up with the best woman a man could ever be so lucky to have look his way. "Thanks. I'm going to go tell Sabrina that she's taking a companion with her to D.C."

They all raised their glasses to him amid calls of good luck. Jonas stepped from the library, glanced out the upstairs windows and caught a breathtaking sight of the Diablos galloping across the back land of the ranch. He stared, knowing they were real, knowing he had taken the journey he'd told his brothers about. They didn't believe him about that—but they did know he was wild about Sabrina.

So surely seeing the mystical, hauntingly beautiful Diablos portended magic one more time.

"ARE YOU SURE THIS IS what you want to do?" Seton asked as she helped her sister pack a bag for little Joe and a suitcase for herself.

"I need to go back. I need to find out if I want to keep my job there, or work somewhere else." Sabrina didn't want to admit that her heart was breaking. Actually, it was completely broken. What would she ever tell little Joe later in life about why she and his father hadn't ever married? What would she do the next time Jonas found a woman he wanted to marry—a woman he really did love, instead of just being friends with, like Chelsea?

Sabrina would have to deal with it. She had to face facts.

"You can do investigative journalism anywhere," Seton pointed out. "It doesn't have to be in D.C."

"I know. I've thought about that. It's better for Joe to be here, with family. I'm not staying there permanently." Sabrina glanced up at her sister before resuming packing. "I just need to get away. It's been really intense ever since I came back for your wedding."

"All the wives are upset that you're leaving. You're part of this family, Sabrina."

"I'll miss them, too." Sabrina sank down on the bed. "My lease is up on my apartment. I need to arrange to move my things back here. I have a complete nursery set up for Joe in my apartment." She smiled. "Ever since he was born, I've been shuttling him between Aunt Corinne's and Rancho Diablo. He's never had a real nursery—not that he needed one. He had a family here." She smiled at her son fondly. If she couldn't have Jonas, at least she had Joe—and that was all that mattered.

"Leave Joe here with me. You can't take care of a baby and pack up an apartment." Seton kissed Joe on the head as he attempted to squirm out of her arms. "He's gotten so busy since he discovered he can pull up and get himself just about anywhere he wants to go."

"I know." Sabrina scooped up the baby. "I can't leave him. I need to spend some time away, and I don't know how long I'll be gone."

"Not long," Jonas said, striding into the bedroom.

"Gosh, I just remembered I left dinner in the oven," Seton said, heading to the door. "I'd best get home and check on it."

"I thought you said you were grilling out tonight," Sabrina said.

"It's a covered casserole. Goodbye!" her sister said, dashing off.

Jonas leaned against the wall, his gaze trained on Sabrina. Joe squirmed mightily, and she realized he was trying to get to his dad. Jonas obliged by coming and taking his son from her arms. She looked at Jonas, wondering why he'd said she wasn't going to be gone long.

"Rafe is going to fly us to D.C. I'm going to help you pack," Jonas said. "And then you and I have some talking to do."

Her heart jumped. "Jonas—"

He held up a hand. "No 'Jonas.' No buts. Sabrina, you belong with me, and I belong with you, and we're a family. All this other bit is just nonsense, not to demean your feelings."

"Well, you are," she said.

"I meant that it's nonsense that I haven't explained to you satisfactorily, and convinced you, how much I love you. But all that comes later."

She waited.

"After we return," Jonas said. "Tonight, we leave in **the family flying carriage.**"

She felt hope dawning irrationally inside her. "You don't have to do this."

"Yes, I do. If I let you get away, you'll think up a thousand more reasons why you can't marry me. I'm not going to ask you again, Sabrina. I realize that asking you to marry me has had a reverse effect from the one I want." He grinned at her. "As much a blow as it is to my pride, I accept that you're unconventional. It's one of the reasons that you're so right for me. Therefore, let me just say that when we return from D.C., we'll get married. But you'll have to ask me, beautiful. I'm not going to do any more of the heavy lifting in this relationship."

Sabrina blinked. "Heavy lifting?"

He nodded. "Just remember, you're going to have to convince yourself that you want me, and you'll have to pop the age-old question next time, my dear."

She wrinkled her nose. "How do you know I will?"

He laughed. "A man can take only so much before he realizes that the woman of his dreams is wired a little differently from others. I wager you'll ask me before this week is out. Don't you think, little Joe?" He kissed his baby on the head, but his gaze stayed on Sabrina.

"And if I don't?" She wasn't certain she liked this new, cagey Jonas.

He shrugged. "I can tell my patients what's best for them, but if they don't want to follow my instructions, that's their choice. It's the old drag-a-mule-to-water thing."

"I resent being compared to a mule."

He waved Joe's fist at her. "Joe says his mom's a

smart lady. He thinks you'll make the right decision for all of us."

Jonas walked out with her son, whistling as he went.

"Be ready to board at oh eight hundred hours!" he called back up the stairs.

"Oh eight hundred indeed." Sabrina tossed some things into her suitcase, wondering how her plans had suddenly gotten sidetracked. He wanted *her* to ask *him* *to* marry her?

"We'll see about that," she murmured, and closed her suitcase, telling herself Jonas was pretty much the proverbial donkey in their relationship. But it didn't escape her that her heart was a whole lot lighter than it had been just twenty minutes before.

EVERYONE CAME TO SEE THEM off at the airport. Sabrina was warmed by all the Callahans, and Aunt Corinne, and even Mavis Night and Nadine Waters, coming to say goodbye.

"Here's something I thought you might need," Aunt Corinne said, handing over a big white box with a beautiful pink bow tied on it.

"What is it?" Sabrina asked, not sure why she'd need a gift for the short trip she was taking.

"Open it and see," Corinne told her.

She took off the bow. Jonas held the box so she could pull out what was inside.

"The magic wedding dress," she murmured, shocked and a little embarrassed that her aunt was so forthright. And yet Sabrina was somehow pleased, too.

Applause broke out from the family, but Fiona gasped.

"Where did you get that, Corinne Abernathy? I've been looking everywhere for it!"

"I bought it." Corinne looked pleased with herself. "I bought it and I put it away for a special occasion for Sabrina. I told Jackie and Darla not to tell a soul, because I didn't want Sabrina to become suspicious. But I wasn't about to let one of those out-of-towners we've been recruiting with our ad campaigns come in and snap it up." She gave Jonas an arch look. "This dress is magic, you know. And Sabrina is the only soon-to-be Callahan who hasn't yet gotten to wear it."

Jonas nodded. "I'm well aware of that, believe me."

"Aunt Corinne," Sabrina said reprovingly, yet she was touched just the same. "Thank you!" She hugged her aunt to her. "I doubt I'll ever get to use it, but if I am married, I want to wear this gown."

Corinne sniffed. "You just might think about wearing it in D.C. I'd hate to miss out on a wedding, but goodness knows, most of the Callahan brides have needed one or two weddings to set the deal in stone."

Everyone laughed. Sabrina put the lid back on the box, unable to look at Jonas. When she finally steeled herself to meet his gaze, he winked at her.

"I know, I know," she said. "I have to ask you."

"Now you just need a groom to be the most beautiful bride Diablo has ever seen," he whispered, and Sabrina waved goodbye to everyone and got on board the family jet.

I do need a groom. I really do.

But she wondered why it was so hard to say yes.

Chapter Sixteen

It took only two days to say goodbye to her old life in D.C., and Sabrina couldn't say she was going to miss it. If anything, the trip back had reminded her how much she'd bonded to Diablo—and to a certain man who'd helped her pack up that life. Rafe had lost himself in the city for two days while Sabrina terminated her lease and settled up bills and packed. Jonas said that his brother had gone to bend the ears of certain congressmen, and had a list of sights he wanted to see.

So she'd packed and Jonas had watched little Joe, and it all felt so strange she hadn't known what to think. It seemed as if she was waiting, and Jonas was waiting, for the right moment.

It was the magic wedding dress, in its box on the seat behind her in the jet, that was making her think constant thoughts of her own wedding. Was it her time to be a bride, and to finally wear it? When her mother had given her the treasured gown she'd gotten from a gypsy in a foreign country, she'd explained how the old woman had assured her the dress was magic. Once you put it on, you knew whether the man you were marrying was the right one, your own handsome prince.

Sabrina didn't need a gown to tell her that Jonas was

the only man she would ever love; there was nothing magical about that. She loved him, and had almost from the beginning. Maybe even in the beginning, once she'd realized he wasn't the rascal his aunt Fiona had painted him and his brothers to be. They'd simply been committed bachelors, each and every one of them.

Now they were confirmed husbands. And Jonas wanted to join them.

Sabrina wanted to be part of his life, too.

"We can live here if you want to," he said. "I could set up a practice in D.C."

She stared at him, astonished. "Why?"

He shrugged and bounced Joe on his knee. "I had a practice in Dallas. I could have one here just as easily, if you like it so much."

"What about Dark Diablo? Isn't that your dream?"

"It was my fallback," Jonas said. "You were there— you know what we were going through. We were never certain if we were going to lose Rancho Diablo or not. I just figured I was playing it safe by having a place we could run the family business, if necessary."

She blinked. "I don't want to live in D.C."

"Okay."

"Do you?"

"No. Too many politicians. Lots of fun things to do, though." He picked up her hand and kissed her fingertips. "I'd like to come back someday, troll through Williamsburg, Richmond, Georgetown. Do all the cool tourist stuff with you and Joe."

She nodded. "That sounds like fun."

He pushed his hat down over his eyes and looked as if he was about to settle in for a nap. Sabrina hesitated, confused. One minute they were talking about some-day sightseeing together as a family, next he was snor-ing into his Stetson. The man was impossible. He was arrogant and impossible and set in his ways....

She thought she heard a lilting song coming from the seat behind her. Sabrina paused, wondering if one of Joe's toys had a musical component she hadn't noticed.

Suddenly, she had the strangest feeling it was the wedding dress. Seton had claimed the gown had a strange call, a melody, that she hadn't been able to get out of her head until she'd finally put it on and said *I do.* The other Callahan brides had said the same thing.

No. That was just a story they told each other, just as the Callahan boys had told each other ghost stories, and later, tales of mystical Diablos. Jonas himself claimed he'd ridden one, but then admitted he didn't know how he'd done it.

The melody wrapped itself around her, a lovely, lilt-ing, tempting call.

"Hush," she said.

"Sabrina!" Jonas pushed his hat back and looked at her curiously. "Did you just tell Joe to hush?"

"No." She shook her head. "Of course not. I wouldn't say that to Joe. Get back under your hat."

He studied her. "Can I get you anything?"

You. You can get me you.

"I'm all right. Just a little tired."

He nodded and retreated under the Stetson. She let out a breath.

She'd feel a lot better when she was back in Diablo.

At least she hoped so.

Durn dress, anyway. Silly fairy tale my mother told me. I never really believed it was magic.

But secretly, she'd wanted to.

"HOW DID IT GO?" SAM asked Rafe as he met the plane.

Rafe shrugged. "No wedding bells."

"I heard that." Jonas put a suitcase by the door of the plane. "The lady was busy doing other things."

Sam picked up the suitcase and carried it down the steps. "We think we might have seen Sonny hanging around."

Jonas walked down the steps, not wanting Sabrina to hear what they were talking about. She was on the plane, bundling little Joe into his carrier and grabbing up toys and baby paraphernalia. He'd intended to help, but first it was important to get the news bulletin Sam was trying to share with Rafe. "You really think you might have seen him?"

Sam tossed the luggage into the van. "We're pretty sure it was him. Before we could get to him, he rode off. But no one else would be trespassing on our property."

Jonas's blood turned chilly. "If I see him, I swear I'll shoot him."

"Believe me, we all feel the same." Sam's eyes behind his shades were unreadable. "But we can't."

Jonas didn't want to think about Joe or Sabrina, or any of the Callahan wives and children, being where Sonny could spy on them. "You'd think he'd give up."

"Obviously, he's certain he's going to find something." Rafe carried Joe with him like a trophy. "He's tenacious, I'll grant him that."

"Who's tenacious?" Sabrina came up behind Rafe, and Jonas's mouth dried out. If anything happened to her, or Joe, it would kill him. He could barely think of it.

"No one," he said briskly.

Sabrina ignored him. "Who's tenacious?" she asked Sam and Rafe.

Both men looked at Jonas with guilty expressions.

"Sonny," they both said.

"Thanks," Jonas growled. "Scare her to death, okay?"

Sabrina shot him an impatient look. "I'm not scared. Sonny is annoying. But he can't hurt me. Or Joe."

They all stared at her.

"Well, we're not Callahans. Why would he?" she asked.

"Okay, now see, that's a problem," Jonas said, and his brothers groaned. "You *should* be a Callahan, damn it!"

"I'll catch up with you later," Rafe said, as Sam got in the van. "I've got some paperwork to turn in, and want to see the plane to the hangar."

Jonas climbed in next to Sabrina and Joe in the back of the roomy vehicle. "Thanks for playing chauffeur, Sam."

"I don't mind being the rat coachman." His youngest brother grinned at them in the mirror. "I've been watching *Cinderella* with the munchkins. The women set up a movie date in the den, and all the kiddoes crowded in. The ladies are planning to build a huge media room in part of the attic. Fiona's picking out the biggest television she can find, for Rancho Diablo's own personal movie theater, I guess."

Jonas couldn't help but laugh. "Nothing's ever going to change."

"Nope." Sam glanced at Sabrina as he pulled out from the airport parking lot. "How was the trip, Sabrina?"

She glanced at Jonas. "I'm glad to close that chapter, actually. Thanks for picking us up."

"No problem."

"You don't think Sonny would ever take one of the kids, do you?" Sabrina asked, and Jonas's blood ran cold as ice.

"Why?" Sam asked. "To make us talk about what he thinks we know?"

"I guess so." Sabrina's face was pale as snow.

"I never thought about it," Sam said.

Jonas hadn't, either. He'd refused to. The thought had hidden at the back of his mind, but he'd dismissed it. Sonny was a ghost, an intruder living on the periphery of their lives, searching for something none of them had. He had to know that. "Sonny is waiting for people who will never return. He knows none of us know anything."

"Except you," Sabrina said softly, and Jonas saw Sam glance at him sharply in the mirror.

"I don't know anything," Jonas said. "I had some kind of hallucination because I was tired or something." He wanted to soothe Sabrina, but she looked at him, not believing him at all.

"Anyway, I'm not in any danger," Jonas said. "Trust

me, I couldn't find my way back if I wanted to. I think Running Bear wanted it that way."

"Maybe we ought to beef up security, Jonas," Sam said. "We've got a lot of kids and a lot of wives now to consider. Most of us are around to keep an eye on things, but there might come a time when we're all out or away."

Jonas didn't want to think about it. He didn't want Sabrina more frightened than she was.

She could obviously read his expression. "Don't worry about me, Jonas," she said quietly, "I won't be at Rancho Diablo. For now, Joe and I are going to stay with Aunt Corinne. At least until things smooth out a little. There's plenty of room there and—"

Jonas turned his face away, unable to bear what he saw in her eyes. She wasn't going to come to him, wasn't going to be his. They passed the billboard of her in the sexy white mini wedding dress as they pulled into town, the *Do You Believe in Magic? Diablo, Home of Romance* pronouncement almost too much for him to bear. He could practically hear his own heart breaking, popping apart into a million sad pieces. He saw Sabrina glance at the sign, then look away quickly.

He knew now. There were just too many hurdles for her to cross. And finally, he understood why she felt the way she did.

Magic and romance had somehow passed them by. Neither of them had believed, and now it was too late.

SAM HELPED UNLOAD EVERYTHING from the van at Rancho Diablo, not saying a word. Sabrina appreciated him not making her feel worse than she did. She needed time, and it was so hard to explain why she was scared. It wasn't just Sonny, or the fact that she was head over heels in love with Jonas, despite knowing that he was only trying to do the right thing by her.

She didn't want the "right" thing. She wanted to be anyone but the woman who'd been hired to bring about his downfall. She'd gotten pregnant, they had a beautiful child, but that didn't mean Jonas would have ever chosen her if Joe hadn't come along.

"I'm going to go now," she told him. "Thanks for helping me pack up my apartment."

He nodded. "Anytime."

She got his meaning. She hesitated for just a moment, wanting to say everything that was in her heart. But when he stared down at her so patiently, so kindly, she found words failing her. He was a kind man. Little Joe was going to grow up and find out that his dad was one of the best men walking the face of the earth, a man among men, a great father. "Thank you," she said again, feeling hopeless, and walked toward the kitchen to say goodbye to Fiona.

It was time.

Though night was beginning to fall, Sabrina was still surprised that Fiona wasn't either outside to greet them, or in her favorite haunt, the kitchen. "Fiona?" she called, flipping on some lights. Jonas had stayed outside with Joe, so Sabrina decided to check the basement. Fiona was often to be found down there with her canning or her extensive collection of twinkling lights and holiday decorations.

Sabrina heard a noise near the back door and turned

to say hello to Fiona—freezing when she realized there was a burglar hiding in the kitchen.

Not a burglar. Sonny.

Her heart jumped in her chest.

He put one finger over his lips in an unmistakable warning to be quiet. She nodded quickly that she understood, knowing he was dangerous right now, and trapped. He hadn't expected them to return from the airport, thought he'd had the place to himself.

Sabrina couldn't breathe. Where were Fiona and Burke? The thought that this horrible man might have harmed them was too much for her to bear. His eyes were locked on her, watching to see if she'd scream or do anything, but Sabrina couldn't have moved if her life depended upon it.

Jonas's deep voice suddenly boomed outside, and Sonny grabbed her, clearly intending to use her as a hostage so he could get away. Sabrina wanted to fight, wanted to get away from him, but he immobilized her by gripping her arm. Fear kept her from doing anything but stumbling after him as he dragged her with him to the back door.

She squeezed her eyes shut for a second, hoping he'd leave her in the kitchen. Her legs trembled and she choked at the dirty smell of the man clutching her arm with steel fingers. "Let me go!" she said.

He growled back, "Shut up if you ever want to see that brat again."

Fear snaked through her and then somehow left her altogether. Maybe she was too afraid to fear dying. All she knew was that Fiona had hired her because of this man, this commando who lived in the canyons, and that he'd intended to kill Sabrina's sister and her husband. And Fiona had known that the easiest way to protect everyone—and Rancho Diablo—was to fill it up with people who loved each other. Love conquered evil.

Sabrina loved Jonas.

When Sonny jerked her out the door to drag her across the drive toward the back of Rancho Diablo, and into the canyons—away from Jonas—Sabrina grabbed the handle of a skillet left on the rack near the kitchen door, fully intending to knock Sonny into the next county. She heard Jonas shout, heard Sam shout, felt Sonny's fingers bite her arm as he jerked her against him for protection. And just as she was about to swing the skillet, a sudden rush of wind and a bone-chilling war cry split the air.

She gasped for breath. Suddenly, Sonny was torn away from her. She whirled around, but all she saw was dust and a black horse and a shadowy rider galloping away, with Sonny being dragged alongside.

Jonas strode to Sabrina, wrapping her tightly in his arms. He took the skillet from her, dropping it to the ground so he could hold her close. She burst into tears against his chest, and Jonas shut his eyes for a moment before staring after the disappearing rider.

"What the hell was that?" Sam demanded, running up with little Joe.

Jonas didn't answer for a long moment. Then he said, "Just a dust devil. Nothing special."

Sabrina looked up at him, and he smiled.

"I don't ever want to be on the wrong side of your frying pan, beautiful. You looked locked and loaded."

"What's going to happen to him?" Sabrina asked.

"There's a lot of things I don't ask Running Bear, and that's going to be one of them," Jonas said, and kissed her on the lips tenderly. "But I've got a hunch we've seen the last of that particular problem."

"Yoo-hoo!" Fiona called, coming out of the barn. "I thought I heard thunder. But it's clear as anything out here!"

Burke followed behind her, his grin broad. "You're back. How was the trip?"

"It's good to be home." Sabrina took a deep breath, then looked up at Jonas. "Jonas?"

"Yes, my cayenne pepper?"

She gave him an adoring gaze that he certainly appreciated. "I didn't plan for this moment, obviously, but I'm officially proposing. Will you marry me?"

He crooked a brow. "What's this? A marriage proposal?"

Sabrina pinched his arm. "I'm one of the Callahan women now. It's time to make an honest man of you."

"Because your frying pan says so?" Jonas teased.

"That's right," she said sweetly. "And now that you're aware I've got great aim, you'd best be a good husband."

"I plan on it," he said, taking her into his arms for a long and loving kiss. He'd waited years for this moment, and as the sun sank on the horizon, Jonas knew that the wait had been worth it. The woman he loved was his, and he was no longer the last bachelor of Rancho Diablo.

Thunder rumbled in the canyons—or at least it sounded like thunder. Dark shadows melted across the horizon, haunting and mystical, a mirage to the eye.

"What is it?" Sabrina whispered. "More dust devils?"

"Diablos. The magic of Rancho Diablo," he said, and raised his arm in a salute to the wild, free rush of dark beauty painting the horizon before slipping away into the endless canyons they called home.

Chapter Seventeen

"We decided that Dark Diablo is the perfect place to open up a second ranch operation," Jonas told Sabrina, the day after the long nightmare had finally ended. "I know you want to live here at Rancho Diablo. So that's my first wedding gift to you."

"Thank you. It means a lot to me. Dark Diablo is beautiful, but this is home." Sabrina smiled at the man she would marry tomorrow. She could hardly wait.

"We've long wanted to open a horse breeding operation. Some of my brothers are itching to branch out. Now that we've settled a lot of the drama around the ranch, we can get started on things we've always wanted to do but never had time for before."

"Not too much time," Sabrina said. "I'm thinking about the pitter-patter of small feet. You know, a brother or sister for Joe."

Jonas smiled, and he was so handsome it took her breath away. "Joe told me he wants several brothers and sisters. We'll have to practice a lot to meet his goals. He thought six might be a real good number."

Sabrina leaned into Jonas, her head on his shoulder, satisfied with his vision for the future. They sat on the porch at Rancho Diablo, looking at the pretty decorations that had been put up for their wedding. Fiona and the BBS had been busy, and Sabrina thought the ranch looked more beautiful than it ever had. "I can't believe we'll be married tomorrow."

Jonas kissed her on the lips, then her nose. "I've been trying to think of a way to make certain you don't get away from me, and the only thing I can come up with is sleeping with you."

"That seems to be your answer for everything," Sabrina said with a laugh. "Lucky for you, Aunt Corinne bought me a wedding nightie."

"Excellent. We'll break it in one night early." He looked pleased at the prospect.

"You know the groom isn't supposed to see the bride the night before the wedding."

"Oh, no," Jonas said, "I gave up on living by traditional rules. Anyway, that rule was not thought up by a man, I can assure you. No groom would think it was bad luck to sleep with his bride the night before the wedding. It's nothing but good luck for me to see you tonight, and it'll be even better luck when I see you in the sexy wedding nightie. I will feel *very* lucky."

Sabrina thought she'd be very lucky, too. In fact, knowing that she was going to be with Jonas for the rest of her life made her feel like the luckiest woman in the world. "I want tomorrow to be here today."

"Eager bride. I like that." Jonas got up, brushing off his jeans. "I have to drive out to Dark Diablo. Wanna ride shotgun, eager bride?"

"I have a thousand things to do...." Sabrina hesitated, but as she stared up at her big fiancé, she decided nothing was as important as being with Jonas.

"Great. I've already asked the Callahan ladies if they'd mind keeping an eye on Joe for us while we take a quick drive."

Sabrina shook her head, following her man. "You know, there will be days when you say jump and I don't."

Jonas laughed. "I don't remember you ever jumping for me. One thing everybody knows about you for sure is that you're an independent firecracker."

"You remember that." Sabrina climbed into the truck, noticing her soon-to-be-husband wore a satisfied smirk. "What have you got up your sleeve?"

"Nothing," he said, but his tone was entirely too innocent. There was no rushing her stubborn surgeon, however, so Sabrina settled in to wait.

She didn't have to wait long.

"Look over at that billboard," Jonas told her on the road out of town. He stopped the truck so she could better view it.

Sabrina stared at the sign that had once shown her holding little Joe and wearing a white, mini wedding gown. Now it read *Do You Believe in Magic? Come to Diablo, a Magical Family Place.* She wore the magic wedding dress in this rendition, and Jonas was painted in beside her, wearing his *Cowboys Do It Better* T-shirt, as was little Joe.

"A vast improvement, I think," Jonas said, pleased. "Don't you?"

"Attention getter," Sabrina stated, loving the new sign ever so much better than the one of her by herself. "You just wanted to be in two billboards."

"I thought I was going to pop a coronary every time I passed that picture of you doing the sexy bride thing,"

Jonas said, wearing a contented expression now that he'd fixed the egregious sign. "As a cardiac guy, and the newest—and only—heart surgeon serving both Diablo and Tempest, I have to take care of my ticker. And that old sign was giving me heartburn every time I passed it. Seeing my woman in that tiny dress with her long legs and great, luscious—"

"That's enough," Sabrina said. She looked at Jonas, secretly proud of him. "So when did you decide to start practicing again?"

"When that billboard went up," he teased as they resumed their drive toward Dark Diablo. "Until I saw you on that sign and realized about a hundred men a day were going to be stopping in town asking about you, I realized that the heart is a very delicate organ. I have great sympathy for the old folks around here. They deserve the best care they can get."

She shook her head, smiling. "I don't believe you. But congratulations, Doctor."

"I'm going to build my own medical building at Dark Diablo. It's going to be a state-of-the-art care center. I'm thinking about leasing out space to other specialists. It's time Diablo and Tempest became known for something other than cowboy hunks."

"And big attitudes. There's no shortage of those around here," Sabrina with a laugh. She was more proud of Jonas than she could say. Little Joe was going to be amazed by what his father could do. "It's a wonderful wedding present, Jonas. Thank you."

He covered her hand with his. "That's not all. But you'll have to wait for the other surprises."

"I have one for you, too," Sabrina said as they, at

long last, reached their destination. "Your aunt has asked Seton and me to take over the running of the Books'n'Bingo Society. Just the tearoom and book area, not the club, of course. No one could replace Fiona."

Jonas grinned. "You're really part of Diablo now. There's no turning back."

"I don't want to turn back." Sabrina gave him a long kiss, pressing her lips against his, wanting to show him how much she loved him. "I don't think I ever did. My place is with you, and Joe."

"Wow," Jonas said. "Hang on, I'll be around there faster than you can blink those beautiful eyes of yours."

She watched him hustle around to scoop her from the truck, jogging with her inside the little farmhouse.

"What are you doing?" Sabrina asked with a delighted squeal. She thought she knew where Jonas was heading—and approved wholeheartedly.

"I want to tell you how much I love you, sweet gypsy," Jonas said. He set her gently on a sofa that still had tags hanging from it, after being delivered yesterday.

"Sabrina McKinley, I love you," he said, going down on one knee. "You drive me mad, in a good way. You've changed my life in a wonderful way. I can't wait for you to be my wife." He handed her a tiny velvet box, and when she didn't open it right away, he pulled it open for her.

Inside was a beautiful, sparkling ring with an oval-shaped diamond.

"Oh, *Jonas,*" Sabrina murmured. "It's so lovely!"

"Put it on. See if it fits," he urged, eager to see his handiwork. "I had it designed in Dallas at Harry Winston's. I wanted something made, so it would be the only one. Because you're a work of art, the only woman I could ever love."

"Jonas," Sabrina said, falling even harder in love, "thank you."

"See, I can be romantic," Jonas said, and she pulled him up beside her on the sofa so she could kiss him.

"I know." Sabrina gazed into his eyes, delighted with her ring and her man's newfound romantic side. "I can be, too, you know."

Jonas waited, obviously caught by the suggestion in her voice. "Oh?"

"Mmm. I've been thinking that your creek might have some magical properties."

"A magic creek?"

"Okay, I don't know about magic," Sabrina said, laughing, "but I do know you made me feel magical when we swam in it. And more."

"That's it," Jonas said. "Get your suit on. We're going in."

They stood, clasping hands, looking at each other with love.

"On the other hand," Sabrina said, "your new bed is pretty magical, too."

Jonas laughed. "I love the way you think, babe," he said, and taking her in his arms, carried her up the stairs.

ON A WONDERFULLY SUNLIT day in Diablo, Sabrina held up the magic wedding dress in front of a mirror, realizing all her dreams were about to come true. Her mother had said that the magic in it was meant to be shared, and so it had to keep moving; Sabrina had assumed the gown would be long gone before she ever found a man she loved enough to wear it for.

But she'd found Jonas. And now this moment of magic was hers. Sabrina slipped the gown on, gasping at her image in the mirror. The dress fit like a dream, as she'd always known it would. And she did see her one true love—Jonas, big and strong and handsome. Not a vision, but the real thing.

At long last, she was home.

"Now, Jonas," said Sam, who was playing best man, "as your most practical brother, I want to share some advice with you. Don't freak out today."

Jonas grinned as Sam struggled with his bow tie. "Freak out about what?" Jonas's own tie had gone on smoothly, his black tux looked good, if he did say so himself, and he was about to marry the most beautiful woman in the world. What was there to freak out about?

"I know you have the worst phobia about altars," Sam said. "But Sabrina isn't Nancy. She's isn't going to ditch you at the altar."

Jonas laughed and shook his head. "Nancy did a good thing with her bride-on-the-run act. We're both a lot better off with how we ended up." He reached over to help his struggling brother fix his tie. "I'd forgotten all about that. It was in my misspent youth, I suppose."

"If you had a misspent youth, the rest of us were hellions. Still and all, today is your day, and I just don't want you getting cold feet." Sam looked pleased that his tie was finally in place.

"No worries." Jonas had nothing to worry about.

He'd slept with Sabrina last night after the rehearsal dinner, enjoying the heck out of the bridal nightie. His little gypsy was crazy about him, and he planned to make certain she stayed that way.

"I'm glad you're so calm," Sam said. "I'm a nervous wreck."

Jonas chuckled. "Why?"

"Because Seton told me that if I didn't make certain you got to the altar, she had a punishment in mind she was sure I wouldn't like." Sam looked properly horrified. "I suspect she was teasing, but I wouldn't want to find out. Life's pretty good in my house, if you know what I mean. So if there's going to be any last-minute freaking out, give me fair warning so I can get my lasso."

"I'm steady as a rock." It was true. Jonas was confident he'd feel even better after the requisite I do's were finally said. He'd waited a long time for this day, and when Sabrina was finally a Callahan bride, Jonas knew he was going to feel like a king.

"So how'd you finally change her mind, anyway? I figured you were never going to convince Sabrina that you were a serious wedding candidate, especially after you got engaged to Chelsea. Who, by the way, sent us a postcard. She and her mother are now in Key West. She says they're having a blast, and thanks for everything." Sam shook his head. "You very nearly dropped the ball, bro, but I admire how you avoided the fumble in the end."

Jonas didn't care about any of that. Sabrina had been destined to be his, and he was destined to be hers. "You overthink things. I had everything under control the whole time."

Sam shook his head. "She turned you down at least three times. I want to know what you finally did right."

Jonas smiled to himself. "I think Sabrina decided she was a true part of the clan when she went after Sonny with the skillet."

"It's a good thing for him she didn't get to use it. Seton says her sister used to play on a softball team, and has a helluva swing." Sam shook his head. "These McKinley women are nothing to mess around with, bro."

Jonas nodded, agreeing wholeheartedly. It was one of the things he liked best about Sabrina—her fearless independence. "Are you ready?"

"I am. Do you need a steadier before we go down? Something to calm your nerves?" Sam asked, clearly having an attack of wedding jitters himself.

Jonas shook his head and looked out the window, seeing the many guests gathering on the beribboned grounds. "I think everyone in town is here."

"No one wanted to miss Diablo's favorite home boy finally going off the market. I heard there were so many tears after the rehearsal dinner last night that Fiona told all the single women she'd host another ball soon to try to find them eligible bachelors."

Jonas smiled. "Nothing's ever going to change with our adorable, determined aunt."

"Matchmaking's irresistible. And Fiona's the best."

It was true. Their aunt and uncle were great at a lot of things, but mostly being the best guardians the Callahan brothers could have ever had growing up. If it hadn't been for Fiona's Grand Scheme, Jonas wouldn't be a surgeon, a father, a husband, a strong Callahan man. "Our aunt *is* the best," he said with a proud smile. "And now do your job, bro. Get me to the altar. The last Callahan is about to ride."

ALL THE CALLAHAN CHILDREN went down the aisle before Sabrina, dressed in their tiny white clothes, proudly dropping pink rose petals on the ground as they walked. It was a parade of shy faces and sweet smiles as they walked toward their fathers, who were standing at the altar as groomsmen. Even Sam Bear and Joe got to go down the aisle, pulled in a tiny white wagon by Aberdeen's eldest niece, Ashley. The two boys didn't carry satin pillows and rings like true ring bearers, but they enjoyed the ride, and sat still like perfect gentlemen.

The Callahan bridesmaids proudly walked behind their children. Sabrina and Seton glanced at each other, sharing a sisterly giggle, before Seton gave her a tight hug and followed the children.

Then Sabrina, with her gaze on Jonas, began her own walk down the aisle. He looked so handsome that she wanted to rush into his arms, but she forced herself to take the measured steps of a bride who knew her man was waiting for her. Everyone murmured and whispered as she went by, and Sabrina heard snatches of "beautiful," and "so pretty," so she knew that the magic was vibrant and alive. She saw their friends, sitting in white chairs on either side of the aisle, and her parents, who'd flown in for the wedding. Her aunt Corinne had scooped Joe out of the wagon and was holding him in her lap. Fiona had rescued Sam Bear, and the two boys looked bemused as Sabrina went by.

All five of Jonas's brothers stood at the altar, with their wives in lovely bridesmaid dresses. Finally Sabrina was standing by Jonas, and he took her hand. The priest began the ceremony.

Something touched Jonas, a spark, maybe even a bit of magic, and he turned to look to the west. In the distance, Running Bear stood with a man and a woman, watching the wedding with happy smiles. They nodded to him—no ghosts, no figment of his imagination, but flesh and blood—and suddenly Jonas knew that Fiona's challenge to them had never been about who would win the ranch, but whether they would remain a family— the ultimate prize—against all odds.

"Look," Jonas told his brothers, and they did. When they realized their parents and grandfather were there, happy and proud of them and their many children, thankfulness swept the Callahans. And the wild thunder Jonas heard wasn't his heart racing, but the sound of the mystical Diablos running free—as they always had, and always would.

* * * * *

All six Callahan brothers are married,
but that doesn't mean the adventure is over!
Look for bonus CALLAHAN COWBOYS *stories,*
THE RENEGADE COWBOY'S RETURN
and THE COWBOY SOLDIER'S SONS,
coming July 2012 and September 2012,
only from Harlequin American Romance!

HEART & HOME

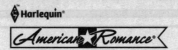

COMING NEXT MONTH
AVAILABLE JUNE 12, 2012

#1405 BET ON A COWBOY
Julie Benson

#1406 RODEO DAUGHTER
Fatherhood
Leigh Duncan

#1407 THE RANCHER'S BRIDE
Pamela Britton

#1408 MONTANA DOCTOR
Saddlers Prairie
Ann Roth

You can find more information on upcoming Harlequin®
titles, free excerpts and more at www.Harlequin.com.

HARCNM0512

REQUEST YOUR FREE BOOKS!
2 FREE NOVELS PLUS 2 FREE GIFTS!

Harlequin

American ★ Romance®

LOVE, HOME & HAPPINESS

YES! Please send me 2 FREE Harlequin® American Romance® novels and my 2 FREE gifts (gifts are worth about $10). After receiving them, if I don't wish to receive any more books, I can return the shipping statement marked "cancel." If I don't cancel, I will receive 4 brand-new novels every month and be billed just $4.49 per book in the U.S. or $5.24 per book in Canada. That's a saving of at least 14% off the cover price! It's quite a bargain! Shipping and handling is just 50¢ per book in the U.S. and 75¢ per book in Canada.* I understand that accepting the 2 free books and gifts places me under no obligation to buy anything. I can always return a shipment and cancel at any time. Even if I never buy another book, the two free books and gifts are mine to keep forever.

154/354 HDN FEP2

Name _____ (PLEASE PRINT) _____

Address _____ Apt. # _____

City _____ State/Prov. _____ Zip/Postal Code _____

Signature (if under 18, a parent or guardian must sign)

Mail to the **Reader Service:**
IN U.S.A.: P.O. Box 1867, Buffalo, NY 14240-1867
IN CANADA: P.O. Box 609, Fort Erie, Ontario L2A 5X3

Not valid for current subscribers to Harlequin American Romance books.

Want to try two free books from another line?
Call 1-800-873-8635 or visit www.ReaderService.com.

* Terms and prices subject to change without notice. Prices do not include applicable taxes. Sales tax applicable in N.Y. Canadian residents will be charged applicable taxes. Offer not valid in Quebec. This offer is limited to one order per household. All orders subject to credit approval. Credit or debit balances in a customer's account(s) may be offset by any other outstanding balance owed by or to the customer. Please allow 4 to 6 weeks for delivery. Offer available while quantities last.

Your Privacy—The Reader Service is committed to protecting your privacy. Our Privacy Policy is available online at www.ReaderService.com or upon request from the Reader Service.

We make a portion of our mailing list available to reputable third parties that offer products we believe may interest you. If you prefer that we not exchange your name with third parties, or if you wish to clarify or modify your communication preferences, please visit us at www.ReaderService.com/consumerschoice or write to us at Reader Service Preference Service, P.O. Box 9062, Buffalo, NY 14269. Include your complete name and address.

A grim discovery is about to change everything for Detective Layne Sullivan—including how she interacts with her boss!

Read on for an exciting excerpt of the upcoming book UNRAVELING THE PAST by Beth Andrews....

SOMETHING WAS UP—otherwise why would Chief Ross Taylor summon her back out? As Detective Layne Sullivan walked over, she grudgingly admitted he was doing well. But that didn't change the fact that the Chief position should have been hers.

Taylor turned as she approached. "Detective Sullivan, we have a situation."

"What's the problem?"

He aimed his flashlight at the ground. The beam illuminated a dirt-encrusted skull.

"Definitely a problem." And not something she'd expected. Not here. "How'd you see it?"

"Jess stumbled upon it looking for her phone."

Layne looked to where his niece huddled on a log. "I'll contact the forensics lab."

"Already have a team on the way. I've also called in units to search for the rest of the remains."

So he'd started the ball rolling. Then, she'd assume command while he took Jess home. "I have this under control."

Though it was late, he was clean shaven and neat, his flat stomach a testament to his refusal to indulge in doughnuts. His dark blond hair was clipped at the sides, the top long enough to curl.

The female part of Layne admitted he was attractive.

The cop in her resented the hell out of him for it.

"You get a lot of missing-persons cases here?" he asked.

"People don't go missing from Mystic Point." Although plenty of them left. "But we have our share of crime."

"I'll take the lead on this one."

Bad enough he'd come to *her* town and taken the position she was meant to have, now he wanted to mess with *how* she did her job? "Why? I'm the only detective on third shift and your second in command."

"Careful, Detective, or you might overstep."

But she'd never played it safe.

"I don't think it's overstepping to clear the air. You have something against me?"

"I assign cases based on experience and expertise. You don't have to like how I do that, but if you need to question every decision, perhaps you'd be happier somewhere else."

"Are you threatening my job?"

He moved so close she could feel the warmth from his body. "I'm not threatening anything." His breath caressed her cheek. "I'm giving you the choice of what happens next."

What will Layne choose? Find out in
UNRAVELING THE PAST by Beth Andrews,
available June 2012 from Harlequin® Superromance®.

And be sure to look for the other two books
in Beth's THE TRUTH ABOUT THE SULLIVANS series
available in August and October 2012.

Harlequin *Romance*

A touching new duet from fan-favorite author

SUSAN MEIER

First Time
D A D S !

When millionaire CEO Max Montgomery spots
Kate Hunter-Montgomery—the wife he's never forgotten—
back in town with a daughter who looks just like him, he's
determined to win her back. But can this savvy business tycoon
convince Kate to trust him a second time with her heart?

Find out this June in
THE TYCOON'S SECRET DAUGHTER

And look for book 2 coming this August!
NANNY FOR THE MILLIONAIRE'S TWINS

www.Harlequin.com

HRI7811

INTRIGUE